M000196381

Stick N Move

A novel

By
Shawn Black

RJ Publications, LLC

Newark, New Jersey

The characters and events in this book are fictitious. Any resemblance to actual persons, living or dead, is purely coincidental.

RJ Publications
Kbwell02@yahoo.com
www.rjpublications.com
Copyright © 2008 by Shawn Black
All Rights Reserved
ISBN 097863733X

Without limiting the rights under copyright reserved above, no part of this book may be reproduced in any form whatsoever without the prior consent of both the copyright owner and the above publisher of this book.

Printed in Canada

January 2008

1-2-3-4-5-6-7-8-9-10

<u>Acknowledgements</u>

First and foremost I would like to give all praises and thanks to the man above **(GOD).** If it weren't for being placed in a situation to where I would have to sit still and wait for you to show me one of the purposes you had destined for me, I wouldn't have been able to see the bigger picture of what you had destined for me. Thank you!

Now, to the ones that stood by me through the stressful times, never turning your backs and always encouraging me to "not let the time do me", I owe you more than you could ever know. Tisha, although I used to beat up on you when we were jits, your big brother had your back. Over the years I've been gone, your call of duty went above and beyond what I ever expected, and I want to let you know that you're the best sister any brother could ever want or have. Those clients of yours can only expect the best when retaining your services.

Ma'Dukes (Gloria), this once ulcer stressful journey is almost over, and without your constant encouragement and steadfast love, I know I wouldn't have gotten as far as I have. Thanks for pushing me and believing in my writing, because without your input and editing on each of my manuscripts I couldn't have conveyed what I wanted the readers to see.

Momma (Rosa Davis), there were many times when I felt that no one thought about, missed, or even cared about me, but you proved that to be wrong. Your constant letters and cards always brightened my day because I felt the love when I read the words you wrote and the scriptures you recited. With you always urging me to keep my eyes on God, I know that's the reason I'm able to be writing acknowledgements. God does bless the ones that has patience and waits on him.

Asia, your Daddy loves you more than you could ever know. Everything I do, the air I breathe, is to be able to ensure a better and brighter future for you. Always remember that no matter how tough the circumstances seem to be, there's always light at the end of the tunnel.

Devon, just as your old man has done, you could do also, even more. The road ahead will be much better for us, but I need you to do your part. Don't follow in my footsteps, create your own, and you'll see that there's enough in the world for everyone. I'm counting on you, Son.

Zaria, your Uncle Sean wants you to know that I love and adore you. I can't wait until we're all together. I'll meet you on the basketball court.

Tameka, Mrs. Sharon, Mr. Milton, and Erika, thank you guys for being a positive and intricate part of my life. The respect, concern, and encouragment you always show me will always be cherished and remembered.

Mona, woman, you've trooped this thing out with me like a rider. Your friendship is immeasurable and I couldn't ask for a better friend. Much love.

The rest of my family: Ced (Big brother), Kim, Mary, Detroy, Frank, Sonny, Jerome, Jeanette, Terri, Honey, Sandy, Audelia, Patrick, Ronald, Howard, Aisha, Tonya, Trevor, Phillip, and if

theres anyone I forgot, my apologies, you will be
added in the next book.

Ms. Tina Hart, you deserve a star of your own. Than
you for reaching out
to help someone you didn't even know. The world need
more good, unselfish, and kind
hearted people. You won't be forgotten, that's a promise!

To my street team and people on the bricks: Big Jap
(Japan), your boy made it. D-mack, I'm looking for that
work real soon, I know it's in stores, Unt and O.G.,
thanks for letting your boy know he wasn't forgotten,
Daron, Sweet-Water, Jay Peace, those Steele sistas out
of Chicago - step for your boy, Twoila, (D. Gainer, my
man from Gator Land, you're the realest), my *boy*
Mitchell J., keep striving, my cuz Shorty (Phillip)- keep
your head up, it's not forever, A.B. you're next in line, J.
Carter (Smoothe), Ben "Money Makin" Adams, Fred,
Mr. Ogle - you're an inspiration, a person I admire and
look up to, your book is going to shed light on a lot of
injustices this government is hiding. My Big Homie Alto
(Tres-four Winston-Salem), and Mark Lowery.

To my best friend, Mo Bass, thanks for always keeping it
real.

Again, If I've missed anyone, my apologies. You will be
included on my next book.

This first book is a dedication to the families; the men
and women that's doing a bid. Always remember, we
are a unique culture and the only way to keep us down
is to keep us contained. Imagine how powerful we could
be!

1

"INFATUATION"

"Scorcher, I'm begging you, please don't go meet with him. Someting's fishy 'bout it. Why after all dis time him just up and decide to meet wid you? Tink 'bout it, you remember what happened to Poncho?" Yasmina begged as her nerves became shot from worrying. She knew if he went to this meeting, it would be the last time she would ever see him alive.

"Baby, no worry, mi got dis ting covered. By the weekend, Kingston will be a ting of the past, we move on to big and betta tings," he replied as he puffed the stick of ganja while listening to the smooth sounds of Gregory Isaac.

Living in Kingston Jamaica for the last three years was enough for Yasmina. Too much was happening and she was tired of what the rugged city had to offer. Although she was born and raised in the ghettos of the city, her heart longed to be back in Miami. Miami held a sense of security, safety, and peace, compared to Kingston. It was becoming more and more dangerous everyday.

Growing up in Tivoli Gardens, Yasmina experienced poverty and death in its entirety. Living with Scorcher, it once again reminded her of how dangerous life was in the impoverished city, and how fortunate she was to have lived in a city such as Miami. It made her remember when she was eleven years-old, and that was something she wanted to forget, forever.

Against the pleading and crying she painstakingly did, Scorcher went ahead with his plans. In the Jamaican culture, a man who did not stand to face his accuser was looked upon as a "battyboy." So with no regards of the ill feelings she continuously warned him about, he stuffed the duffle bag with guns, ammunition, and other necessities. Fearing that death would be the only one to prevail, Yasmina begged him to leave on the plane with her and never look back. Set in his ways, Scorcher was determined to settle his business with Shotty Dread once and for all.

Yasmina and Scorcher had met by coincidence in May of 1999. SPRING BLING was being held in Miami's South Beach that year. The temperature steadily ranging in the mid 90's, was notice enough to the thousands of college students that covered the beautiful beach. A host of entertainers performed, giving the excited crowd plenty reasons to drop it like it was hot. Eve, Ruff Ryders, Snoop Dog, The Hot Boys, Jay-Z, DMX, and a slew of other rappers and R&B singers made their presence felt.

Wanting to be there in their grandest, Yasmina and Selena embarked on making a statement. They wanted to be the main attraction. This meant their clothing was going to cover as less as possible, and they were going to be the eye-candy that attracted the attention of every baller within the vicinity of the beach.

In Miami, there was always something to get into. And for this reason, Yasmina loved it. Coming from Jamaica at the young age of eleven, she despised any and everything about the place, at first. Home was in Kingston, and it was where all of her friends were. It was also a place of refuge for her.

7

Just as Americans celebrate the fourth of July, August 6 was a special day that was celebrated across the island of Jamaica. It was Independence Day. 1961 was a sad year for Jamaicans across the entire island. A lot of innocent people lost their lives because of the tyranny of the government. Being that the People's National Party and the Jamaican Labor Party were at war, the government helped in increasing the bloodshed by providing each group with weapons to kill each other off. The wars were fought in the streets of Kingston, and the innocent perished just as well as those engaged in the horrific massacre. The western parts of the city-known as the ghettos-were burned and looted. And those who lived in the ravaged area, stomped through the upper and middle class neighborhoods, robbing, murdering, and creating chaos throughout the city.

Yasmina grew up in the gutter where poverty and murder went hand in hand. People who lived in Tivoli Gardens, Concrete Jungle, Greenwich Town, Trench Penn, and Rema Housing were uncontrollably mad. All hope for having some sort of a future vanished as the government helped in deteriorating the core of the city. In an effort to survive, the residents had to thrive on other well-to-do people. It was all they could do to survive. During the Independence Day celebration of 1980, the people celebrated in happiness. Once again they'd vanquished their rights back from the government, and things were looking up for them. What was supposed to be a happy day, turned out to be one of the worst days of Yasmina's life. Her mother and father had just left the recording studio. He'd recorded an album called "Upstanding" in tribute to defeating the oppressor. It was going to secure a deal with a company out of New York, but before that night was over, death would have its way.

As the mini-van-taxi cab drove along the quiet, dark, and trash strewn street, two assailants wearing bandanas over half of their faces approached the vehicle as it stopped at a red-light in Trench town. This night commemorated the night of the celebration of Independence, but for the occupants inside, it was something different. Seeing the men yield two automatic weapons, which were later found to be AK-47 Assault Rifles, Yasmina's father frantically ordered the driver to flee the scene. However, a few seconds too late, the only thing that could be heard were the terrifying sounds of people inside the van screaming as bullets tore into the metal-shredding it as if it were a piece of paper. When the assailants let off their triggers, smoke drifted from their hot barrels and the sounds that once came from inside the van were now covered with blood, killing everyone.

Upon receiving the horrible news, Yasmina's grandmother immediately boarded a plane to Kingston. After burying her parents, Yasmina and Rosa flew back to Miami. It would be where Yasmina would start her new life. Now, years later, this was another reminder to her about how bad life in Kingston was. Thoughts of her past flooded her mind as she listened to Scorcher and what he was about to do. He was going to tell Shotty Dread that he was out the drug game forever. And hearing this made her dread the fact that she may be losing someone else she loved dearly, because there was no way Shotty Dread was going to let him walk away that easily.

2

"STARTING FRESH"

It was Yasmina's first year at The University of Miami (U of M). She majored in Accounting, and Marketing as a Minor. Ever since she was young, she had been good with numbers, and this earned her an Academic Scholarship and a free ride to the university. Taking advantage of the gift, she prided herself on being the best at whatever she persued, and this would prove true in the long run.

One day while on campus as a Pep Rally ensued, she kept getting bumped from behind. The Kappa's were in the middle of a step-show, and the constant hitting was beginning to irritate her. "The Show," the rap song that Slick Rick and Doug E. Fresh mastered, was booming out the loud speakers, and entranced by what she was seeing, Yasmina really didn't feel like being bothered. Turning around to confront the person, she noticed a girl full of glee, dancing and cheering the brothas on as they stepped. The thought of smacking her beside the head crossed her mind, but she figured that the bumps were not intentional. Besides, she couldn't afford to blow the free-ride she was getting at school because her grandmother would kick her ass.

"Girl, those Kappa's are doing their thang, aren't they?" said the girl named Selena, as she continued to bump and prod Yasmina on the shoulder. "And they are fine as hell too, girl!"

Yasmina wasn't really feeling the annoying girl as she irritably answered, "Yeah, it's ai'ight, but I would enjoy it more if you weren't breaking my damn arm all day." She was being sarcastic.

Smiling and showing the silver braces that covered the bottom and top layers of her teeth, Selena reached her hand out in a display of friendliness, "My name's Selena, are you from around here?"

At first, Yasmina wasn't about to shake her hand. She was still upset about being nudged to death, but realizing that Selena was being genuine, she accepted, giving her name in return.

"Name's Yasmina, but you can call me Yas for short. I'm from Jamaica but I've been living here in Miami since age eleven. Where are you from?"

"I'm from New York, the Bronx," Selena replied, letting the potency of her accent back her words up.

From that moment on, the two became friends. As if they'd known each other for years, never saw, without the other in tow. This would mark both Yasmina and Selena's first Spring Break as college students, and the excitement had them going crazy. With the event being held in South Beach, they planned on getting their swerves on in immeasurable fashion.

That week, Yasmina and Selena hit every shopping boutique located on the strips between Ocean Drive and Washington Avenue. Gucci, Dior, Prada, Channel, Dolce Gabana, and a host of other expensive shops lined the streets, and each one received a donation from the girls. Though they both were jobless, it didn't hinder them from spending money, or for that matter, someone else's money. Learning how to survive early on, on the huge campus, Yasmina and Selena adopted a creed. "If they're willing to give, we're willing to take."

11

It was a way of survival, and the assets they both possessed were collateral enough.

Yasmina stood at 5'9, 140 pounds, thick-robust hips, and an almond skin-tone that's reminiscent of a cross between Gabrielle Union and Buffy the Body. Selena, an inch shorter, bore hazel eyes, long-silky, jet-black hair that naturally curled to her shoulders, a high yellow complexion-blemish free, and almost the exact build as her protégé, Yasmina. When it came to men, there wasn't a problem. Every athlete and baller around campus wanted them. There were even a few females that lusted after them.

"Look at all these fine ass brothas walking around with their shirts off showing their muscles," Yasmina said as she walked around the beach in excitement.

"Girl we gon' get paid out this bitch 'cause it's too many ballers out here for us not to. Did you see all the Lexus, Mercedes, and Bimmers sitting on chrome? And what about the brotha pushin' the Hummer? He was too-too fine," Selena said in awe of the car show and the fashion show that was unveiling right before her eyes.

"Did I?" replied Yasmina, "Shit. I'm planning on driving my own Mercedes one day, and it'll be paid for and wrapped in a red ribbon by one of these ballers out here one day." She gave Selena a high-five, and both girls started laughing.

"I know that's right," Selena replied, feeling her new friend. "Damn! Let's get a little closer to the stage, sounds like Mary J. Blige is doing something big." Selena practically dragged Yasmina through the raging crowd of spectators that was watching the show.

"Sitting here, wondering why you don't love me, and I know the reason why, but baby have no fear..."

As the words vibrated over the crowd, causing every male and female to dance and croon in rhythm, a few girls clad in skimpy bathing suits sat on the broad shoulders of the shirtless males and hummed the words to the song.

As everyone screamed, cried, and pumped their hands in the air, Selena and Yasmina were enjoying themselves. They knew this would be a Spring Break that would have a lasting memory on them, and they were submersed in the heart of it. But during the performance, Yasmina kept feeling something hard rub her ass. Enjoying herself and realizing how crowded the area was, she shrugged it off, kept dancing and having a good time. When the next song came on, she noticed that the person behind her started rubbing something hard against her once again. Feeling a need to put it to an end, she spun around and was stunned at what she saw. The tall-dark brotha with the locks that reached the length of his back was staring deeply into her eyes. Instincts told her to curse him out, but an attraction that was hard to fight told her differently. As she looked over his well defined body, tingles started running through her body. The potent hydro that she and Selena smoked prior to making it to the beach didn't help in standing firm on her intentions. Yelling over the music the guy asked.

"What's your name?" his deep Jamaican accent was very noticeable.

"Yasmina," she responded, yelling loud over the music. They shook hands and continued talking.

"I'm Scorcher. I'm from Kingston, Jamaica," he explained as if Kingston was a place that was unheard of.

"Oh yeah, I'm a Yarde also. I used to live in Kingston. I moved here some years back." She let her Jamaican accent be known for the first time.

After hours of sweating from the atrocious heat from the sun, the show ended. People started dispersing all over the beach. Some ventured to stripclubs and the bars that aligned it, others went and cooled off in the pools at the hotels, or remained on the beach. Whatever they did, it was South Beach, and what happened in South Beach, stayed in South Beach.

Since the fun Yasmina and Selena were having came to an end, they decided to go back to her grandmother's house. More events were going to be held the next day, so it meant more partying and prospecting for the entire week. Now that she was a freshman resident in the city of Miami, Selena decided to spend her first spring break there. New York would have to be put on the backburner. Besides, Miami will be her home for the next couple of years.

Before they could make it off the beach, they were accosted.

"Y'all wan' come to my hotel room?" Scorcher asked not wanting the two young ladies to leave.

"Damn nigga, do we look that easy? Just because I dance with your ass doesn't mean I'ma fuck you, damn!" Yasmina angrily said.

"My apologies, sistas. Mi meant no harm, maybe mi should've clarified myself a little betta. Mi was only saying that mi have some good ganja and wanted to get to know more about you. That's all."

"Humph, I was just letting you know that it ain't that kinda party." Yasmina rolled her eyes.

After hearing the apology, Yasmina felt like shit. She was so used to guys being disrespectful that she assumed Scorcher was doing the same. After the explanation he gave, she knew he was only being friendly. But then again, she had to let him know where

14

things stood even though they accepted the invitation to his hotel room. Seeing him jump into the all black Hummer that sat on chromed 24 inch rims, they knew at that moment he was balling out of control.

"Day'um!" Selena said aloud. "That's the brotha we saw earlier."

"Excuse me, Ms. Thang, uh, but I'm not blind." Yasmina tried concealing the fact that she was just as excited.

"I wonder if he has any friends?" Selena blurted out, knowing that Yasmina was interested in her catch.

"I can tell he's a big baller by the way he finessed you. Had you creaming in your pants; don't think I didn't notice." Selena laughed, smacking her on the arm.

Going into the hotel reminded Yasmina and Selena of a castle. They've been inside hotels before, but none like the Fountain Bleu. This was the hotel that famous people went to, and it blew their minds. They just knew Scorcher kicked out every bit of a thousand dollars a night for a room. This had both of them wet.

"Girl, I'm in heaven!" said Yasmina. "Can you believe we're in the muthafuckin' Fountain Bleu? Damn, this nigga has to be into some serious shit, you hear me."

Entering Scorcher's suite, Yasmina yelled, "Selena!" It was all she could do when she saw Selena bolting for the Jacuzzi that sat in the middle of the floor. It happened so fast and unexpectedly, the only thing she could do was cover her mouth.

"Oh My God, Scorcher," Yasmina said looking at him, "I'm sorry. I mean I apologize, I didn't know she was gon........"

"No worry," Scorcher placed a hand on her arm-letting her know everything was fine. "Enjoy yourselves. Mi just wan' the both of you's to have a good time. Plus, mi wan' know more about you Ms. Yasmina from Kingston." He smiled.

Sitting in the apartment size suite, the three talked about any and everything as they smoked the ganja that Scorcher told them about. After a while, Yasmina started getting the munchies. When room service arrived, the women were ecstatic. Shrimp platters and Moet were served. It was like a fairytale to Yasmina as she savored the taste of the shrimp and the expensive bottle of champagne. Only stars lived like this.

After the mouth-filling scrumptious meal, Scorcher told them a little about himself. He told them about the importing/exporting business he runs. He shipped exotic fruit from Jamaica to the U.S. He had a hand in a couple of real estate ventures, and he was a music promoter. Hearing these things burned holes in the ears of Yasmina and Selena. Ch-ching! They knew they'd definitely hit the jackpot.

During the conversation, Yasmina wondered to herself about his age. He didn't look a day older than twenty-three, and it was confirmed later when he told her his age. He was twenty-four. All this news and information was too much for Yasmina to take in. In so, she got out her chair and went into the bathroom. Her juices were now boiling. Here she is, a freshman, netting a twenty-four year old rich baller that owned beaucoup businesses. At the thought, all kinds of things ran through her head. She could vividly imagine herself running her nails through his thick locks as his sweaty muscle-ripped body pounded her insides. She could see herself pregnant with his child, she could see herself dr........"

"Yasmina!" Selena yelled as she pounded on the door, breaking Yasmina out of her stupor.

"What?"

16

"You have your two-piece on under your sundress , don't you? Let's hop into the Jacuzzi and do like some real ballin' bitches will do." Selena came out of her Prada Skirt and unveiled a bathing suit that matched.

The day before all the events started, Yasmina and Selena drove up and down Ocean Drive, Washington Avenue, and Collins Avenue, trying to find some cute outfits to wear. They knew all the other females were going to be sharp, so they had to be even sharper. That meant going for the best. Even though the sun was going to be stifling hot, it wasn't going to deter them. Yasmina found a Gucci-mini skirt with a wife beater that had "G" placed nicely in the center, then purchased a pair of leather Gucci Sandals to match. Two more outfits completed her weekend wardrobe. Selena, having different taste than Yasmina, purchased three outfits that were of eloquence but bore the name of some other designer she probably would never meet in her life. But they were just as hot as Yasmina's. The clothing they planned on wearing was going to make a fashion statement, and whoever the catch was, would have to realize that he wasn't getting his hands on some normal chickenhead.

Yasmina, clad in the Gucci-two piece, stepped out the bathroom like a model strutting the runway. Her legs were polished and glistening, and her curves were magnified by ten. Scorcher, completely thrown off, had to do a double take. His eyes almost popped out the sockets. Seeing the flawless body stand before him with the toenails and fingernails matching the bathing suit, was unbelievable. He knew she possessed beauty, but to see her in this light was something out of this world. She was phat-to-death. Walking toward the Jacuzzi, Yasmina

17

gave her "look at what could possibly be yours" attitude, as she gracefully stepped into the warm-bubbly water. Before sitting down, she knowingly turned around, bent over, and gave him a booty shot. That was the tease that put the icing on the cake.

"Girl, you need to stop," Selena said laughing. "I saw the extra twist and umph you added to your walk when you saw him drooling over himself." She splashed water on Yasmina.

"You know how we do it girl, we came to play. Now pass me that joint 'cause your ass is holding it a little too long. You know, puff-puff give!" they both burst out laughing.

The day seemed to fly by. Before they'd realized it, it was going on nine o'clock. And they were having the time of their lives. Contemplating on what to do next, Yasmina was about to ask Selena if she was ready to leave. It was getting late, and she knew her grandmother was probably worried. She hadn't called her since leaving the house.

Deciding now was as good a time as ever, Scorcher made his next move.

"I'm heading to Club Level in a few, if you guys wan' roll wit' me, my friend owns it and you can join me in the V.I.P, if you like. Everyting' on me." He stood with his hands open-palms flat.

For this one, Yasmina and Selena had to consult with each other, and what better place than the bathroom. Plus, it was hard to conceal the excitement that was running rampantly through them.

"Yas, that nigga is major. I mean ballin' like a muthaf…"

Placing a hand on Selena's arm, Yasmina interrupted her comment.

"I know he is, but we still can't show him that we're too impressed. We gotta keep playing our trump cards. You know, make him think that we've done this before and it ain't nothing new to us." She sprayed a tad of Vera Wang Perfume between her breast and a little on her panties and then applied the clear lipstick that made her lips even more luscious.

Little did Selena know, Yasmina was as excited as she was, if not more. They'd been doing the club scene a couple of months and never once heard about Club Level. The clubs they frequented were in the hood. Those were the spots where all the ballers they knew hung out, not South Beach. The moment they stepped into the club, was like a time warp. Everything slowed down basically coming to a halt, and they noticed every guy staring at them. The line outside the club was unbelievable in itself. It extended down the entire block. Luckily, the bouncer didn't even blink twice when Scorcher walked ahead of everyone and led them into the club. Free. The sneers and insults could be heard by others who'd been waiting for hours to get in, but was overshadowed as the bass from the music severed everything. As if walking down the red carpet, a spotlight found them as the DJ gave Scorcher a big shout-out. Heads turned, and out of nowhere, people started walking up to him giving him dap. It's like he was a movie star, Yasmina thought to herself. She couldn't believe the recognition he was getting. This bugged both her and Selena out.

"Damn, did you hear the big shout-out the DJ gave him? And what about all the people running up to him? For a minute, I thought Denzel was in here or something," she whispered to Selena.

19

The words Yasmina spoke went unheard. Selena was in her own world. She was too consumed with the people staring in their direction, and the glares they were getting from the jealous women. Making it to the V.I.P, they were shocked at who they found inside. DMX, Jay-Z, and EVE were sipping on some bubbly and relaxing. Each one had a bottle of Dom Perignon and a bottle of Louis XIV chilling on ice.

Once again Selena was speechless. The entire time they were in the presence of the superstars, she sat dumbfounded. Although she sipped on some champagne offered to her by EVE, she didn't speak one word. For Yasmina, she was on cloud nine. The praise he was getting from people was unbelievable. She loved the fact that she was his date, even if only for one night.

"Selena, Selena!" Yasmina nudged her shoulder. "You ai'ight?"

"Huh, oh yeah. I'm just trying to stay in this dream as long as I can. Don't wake me up, alright?" Everyone fell out laughing.

On their way to the club, Yasmina figured they were going to dance. That's how her and Selena did it when they went to the clubs in the hood. They would either sit at a table and wait on some baller to buy them drinks, or they would head straight to the dance floor and get their party on. For them to be mingling amongst real bonafide ballers had them ecstatic. They were on top of the world.

EVE, Jay-Z, and DMX left the room shortly afterwards, but not before letting

Yasmina and Selena know how much they enjoyed their company and invited them backstage at the show the next day.

In her excitement, Yasmina screamed to herself after they left, "Did you hear them invite us backstage tomorrow?"

"Hell yeah, we da' shit! We da' shit!, it's your birthday!" it's your birthday!" Selena sang as she did the Cabbage Patch.

"Go 'head, go 'head, go, go, go," Yasmina cheered her on as she joined in on the dance.

After leaving the club, Scorcher informed the girls that they were welcomed to stay in his hotel room. It was late and he felt like they should rest before driving back across town. He even went as far as saying that he'd rent another room so they wouldn't feel uncomfortable. Declining, Yasmina told him that she'd already told her grandmother that she would be coming home; regretting that she did. Before departing ways, she made sure to get his cell-phone and hotel number. With that done, she hesitantly walked over to him, looking him directly in the eyes, and placed a long, juicy-wet kiss on his lips. Selena practically had to drag her out the room.

While driving back to Carol City, they popped in Eve's c.d. and jammed to, "Who's that Girl," while rapping the lyrics word for word.

"I'll never forget this night," Selena said turning the volume down.

"Me either. I'll tell you one thing too, your ass was about to be sleeping in the other room. If I would've kissed him a second longer, we would've been fucking tonight." She laughed and gave Selena the pound.

3

Anticipation

A few moments later, the plane skidded on the runway leaving the fresh air smelling like rubber as it came to a stop. The screeching of the tires didn't bother Yasmina. What worried her was Jamaica. As the plane descended in altitude across the crystal-clear blue waters, her heart pounded furiously. The anticipation of seeing Scorcher made her nervous, but the fact that she hadn't been back to Jamaica since her parents' death, frightened her. She really didn't know how it was going to affect her, she thought to herself as she took deep breaths.

It had been over two months since she last saw Scorcher. The last time they were together was during spring bling, and it was a memory that wouldn't let her rest. For most people, first impressions are everything. And the impression he left embedded in her mind wouldn't go away.

Being invited backstage by Eve and Jay-Z was enough in itself to satisfy Yasmina, but Scorcher took it to the next level. Calling his cell phone, she didn't get an answer. She assumed that she figured him wrong. "He's just like every other guy. Out to get the pussy," she told Selena when she kept getting voice mail. Surprised, the phone rung back immediately and it was him on the line. After talking and deciding where to meet, the date was set. In their matching Dior Skirts, Yasmina and Selena was every bit of a thousand dollars together. That didn't include the six inch-stiletto pumps by Jimmy Choo.

Anyone who saw them that day couldn't help but to do a double take, because they were more than hot. They were on fire.

To ease the mind of Selena, so she wouldn't feel like three's a crowd, Scorcher had something in store for her, Murray. He brought Murray, his friend and business partner along. Not knowing whether they would connect, he was surprised. From the moment they laid eyes on each other, it was an instant attraction. This made the night go along smoother, and everyone was relaxed. Since it was going to be his last night in town, he really wanted to make it a night to remember. Being the smooth player he is, dinner was held atop of the hotel, where only the four could attend. As the breeze blew off the beach, they ate by candlelight as a violinist serenaded them with music. For Yasmina, she wished the night didn't have to end.

It was the first time she'd ever had a guy be a complete gentlemen to her, and it felt different. What she liked about him was his character. Laid back, smooth, and calculated. Although he seemed a little too casual, she knew there was another side to him. A roughneck thug hidden somewhere, and she planned to find it, because every woman wants a roughneck-some of the time.

The first week after she went back to Miami, Yasmina was a wreck. She constantly moped around the dorm not wanting to do anything except wait by the phone. There were certain hours he would call her, and she dare not miss him. Selena couldn't get her to budge. She tried her best at getting her old friend back, you know, the wild, outgoing, outspoken Yasmina, but to no avail. This is when she really started noticing how bad Yasmina had it. One of their favorite money giving male friends was in the mood to come off of some hard earned cash. This was an opportunity for both Yasmina and Selena to recoup some of what they'd spent at spring bling. When Selena mentioned it to Yasmina, she acted as if she didn't hear a word of what Selena had to say. Now this really had Selena looking deeper at her friend. The old Yasmina she knew loved three things, and three things only, money shopping and good dick. For her to turn Darren down, she had to have fallen hard for Scorcher, Selena summed up. The bad thing about it was, they didn't have to sleep with Darren. He'd watch them do a little striptease in the privacy of their room, and then he'd go into the bathroom and masturbate. They would come off like phat rats, and everyone would be happy. For this to be happening, Selena knew she had to do something, and fast.

While Yasmina stood under the roof of the airport, hiding from the sun, the thoughts she had on the plane came flooding back to her. But there were more things she had to deal with now.

Scorcher was rolling up the parking lot in a midnight blue 2000 Mercedes Benz. Seeing this made her knees weak, and for a second she buckled. She knew he was really showing her his player card, and she loved every minute of it. Now this was something she couldn't wait to tell Selena.

"Aye beautiful," he said getting out of the car with a smile on his face. "Ya been waitin' long for me?" he pressed a button on the hand held remote control, causing the trunk to click, then hiss as it slowly opened up. He grabbed her bags and put them in. This blew her mind.

"Nah, I just came out the door right before you pulled up. I needed some fresh air, jet lagged-you know."

Scorcher then gave her a hug and placed a soft kiss on her lips. This instantly caused her nipples to get hard and her juices to flow. The cologne he wore didn't help deter her naughty thoughts.

"You wan' get something' to eat? Mi know dis' place that has the best Curry Goat and Red Beans and Rice on the island. Afterwards, mi take you to see your old home, Tivoli Gardens."

"Ai'ight, only because I want to see how much the place has changed," she replied with a hint of sadness even though she wanted to go.

Every time she thought about Tivoli Gardens, her parents came to mind. Although they'd been dead for seven years, she missed them like it was yesterday. It was still hard on her. The only real memories she possessed were some pictures they'd taken. She could vaguely remember dancing with her mother while her father and his band practiced.

"Shaw'ty, you alright?" Scorcher asked sensing something was wrong. Snapping out of her reverie, she answered, "Yeah I'm fine."

They wined at this restaurant called Paradise Island, Yasmina ordered Ox Tails and he ordered curry goat, and they were the best she'd ever tasted. After eating a fulfilling meal, they left. Since she saw firsthand how he flossed in Miami, she wanted to see if his game was airtight in Jamaica as well. Yasmina knew brothas could put on good fronts to impress a lady. If he was truly ballin', this would put him to the test, she thought as the cool air blew in her face.

"So, you're really from Tivoli Gardens, huh?" asked Scorcher.

"Born and raised," she responded. "What about you? Where are you from?"

"Trench Town, yup' that's mi home. It's rough there though. Poverty has the place by it's throat, but mi managed to make it out by the grace of Hallie Salasie."

At hearing the words "Trench Town", she went into a shell. He was from the same terrible place where her parents had lost their lives. Still melancholy, she sat quiet the rest of the trip through the raw heart of the ghetto. While riding, Yasmina couldn't believe the sight. Things still looked the same as when she lived there. Shanty villages barely stood, slummed buildings, and cardboard boxes aligned the streets; used as shelter for the homeless.

Going back to Yasmina's old stomping grounds wasn't quite as she remembered it. Before she left, in the eyes of a child, it was beautiful. Now it looked to be what was the center of a big war zone. A very drab scene. Burnt out buildings stood in vacant lots, tires, junk cars, refrigerators, and debris scattered the once front and back lawns of homes. Seeing this sight wasn't beautiful anymore, and she finally realized why her parents were trying to move. They wanted a better way of life.

Yasmina's mood had dropped to an all-time low, and Scorcher could tell that she was bothered by something. Knowing he wouldn't understand the reason behind her sadness, she pretended like everything was okay. Many times she wanted to ask him if he'd heard about the incident with her parents, but decided against it. Some things were better left alone, and this was one of them.

The Mercedes cruised through different parishes and Yasmina could see the drastic changes that Kingston underwent. After reaching her neighborhood, she could see the metal and cement gate that surrounded part of the entrance. Scorcher stopped the car so they could take a closer look, she could see her hand print and names written in black ink, although it was partially covered by weed and vines. That's when memories of her past surged through her with tremendous forces. A vacant lot now stood where she once lived. Part of the house was still standing, but the other part was in ashes. Now it was being used by the homeless. Having seen enough for one day, she was ready to leave. The image of the torn-down tornado infested place wasn't what she wanted to remember her parents by. They deserved better than that.

"You live here all by yourself?" Yasmina asked after pulling up to the huge home that was surrounded by an electronic gate that posted a guard in a booth.

"True, just myself," Scorcher smiled.
For a brief moment she was speechless. She couldn't believe this young twenty-four year old baller was doing it like this. "A Mansion!" she said to herself. As they made it closer to the center driveway, she could see a few vehicles parked. A Lexus 300, a Toyota Sequoia sitting on chrome, and a Porsche 911 Carerra. She couldn't name it, but she knew it was expensive. As they made it inside the luxurious home, the first place Yasmina stopped was the kitchen. She knew if the house was like that, then the kitchen had to be off the chain. And she was right. Her eyes didn't focus on anything in the kitchen, they went straight through the window. Outside she could see a pool filled with blue water, but even better, the pool turned out to be the ocean. It was the same aqua blue waters that she flew over. Putting two and two together, she knew it was more exciting to her.

After being dazzled, Yasmina felt tired. It was a long day, and some of the things she saw weren't sitting well with her. Weary and still kind of jet-lagged, she decided to take a nap. When she closed her eyes, darkness swallowed her like a black hole.

4

"WHAT?"

Awaking early the next morning, Yasmina found herself covered under one of the softest blankets she'd ever felt. Reading the tag stitched to it, she almost screamed aloud. It was a Chinchilla Fur Blanket. Fascinated by the smooth texture it possessed, she snuggled it to her body and smiled.

Not clearly remembering but quite sure of herself, she didn't recall Scorcher sleeping in the bed with her. This was a shock. She knew the flight wore her out, but she didn't mean to waste the day away by not showing him any attention. In fact, the only thing Scorcher did do was place the fur over her. He knew she was drained, plus he had a few calls to make. There was some business that needed to be discussed with Shotty Dread.

Sitting atop the bed, Yasmina thought back to the dream she had. In a way she was glad that Scorcher didn't sleep with her. All night, she tossed and turned violently. She'd been having these same dreams since her parents were killed. While dreaming, chills ran down her spine. She could see the horrific expressions on her parents' faces as they desperately tried crouching from the gunfire. Seeing the weapons being aimed and the bullets flying out the muzzle, caused her to shake and turn while she slept. Finally awake, she was drenched with sweat and constantly sniveled, as tears trickled down her brow. Since Scorcher was nowhere to be found, she made her way into the huge bathroom. She

29

needed to regroup and present herself in a jolly mood because today is a different day, and the past needed to remain as that, the past.

As the day went on, Yasmina and Scorcher had done so much that time seemed to slip by on them. She had only three days left in Jamaica, and it was back to Miami. Summer break was over and the next school semester was starting. She wanted to be back early enough to get prepared for her sophomore year in college. This was a big achievement and it meant no more orientations, no pre-college elective courses, and no more being looked down upon.

Out of the two days of being in Jamaica, Scorcher hadn't as much made the slightest inclination that he was interested in Yasmina sexually. This puzzled her. The kiss at the airport didn't count. It's human instinct to make a gesture of such. With him not sleeping in the same bed as her the entire time she'd been there, left her mind wandering. The night before she left to go back to Miami, as bad as she wanted to make love to him, she didn't. Not because of her, it was him. He didn't make any moves or react to her signals. Now, this left her thinking bad things about him. For the past couple of nights, he slept in one of his guest rooms. She desperately wanted him to snuggle up to her under the chinchilla fur, but she wasn't going to be the aggressor. When it comes down to situations as such, women shouldn't have to be that aggressive. Especially the ones with class, she thought to herself.

Seeing Scorcher walk around at night in his silk-Gucci Pajamas; his shirt off, and hair pulled back, did things to Yasmina. For starters, it mad her moist between the legs. Even when she would walk in on him exercising, while he did his push-ups, every muscle in his back would appear and his tight butt cheeks would standout, she'd get wet. Seeing this, she would imagine him using the same movement as he stroked her tenderly. When he did his abs, she would imagine herself riding him. And when he did pull-ups, his dick print stood out all too well in the silky thin material. This made her want to rape him. She had to be strong. Besides, her Platinum Player Card was just as valid as his.

As it would happen, the torture was beginning to become too much. The mere thought of sexing him caused her to become moist, more than once. In order to quench her thirst, she had to resort to alternative methods. As her idle mind went to places of fascination, her hands drifted slowly under the soft chinchilla fur, until they reached paradise. At first ashamed, the friction and moistness engulfed her fingers-spurring her to delve deeper into satisfying her burning desire. With the crinkled sheets ruffling over her body, she writhed in ecstasy as her fingers caused her to jolt. The pleasure was beginning to overtake her as she dug deeper and deeper, trying to reach that point where she could exhale. Finally making it there, she bit into the blankets, letting out a stifled cry, then fell asleep, although not fully satisfied.

Spanish Town was a diverse part of Kingston where the nightlife was enjoyed by people of all walks of life. Clubs and café's aligned the well lit streets. This was the good part of the city.

Being that time was getting short, Scorcher planned a special day for Yasmina. He knew she wanted him sexually, and he wanted the same, but he wanted more from her. Of course, sex was important to him, but he wanted to show that he was not the typical guy, unlike other men she had probably dated. With him, sex wasn't going to determine their relationship, if there would be one. After arriving at a West Indian Café called Me'yard, Yasmina was impressed. They were escorted to a table where the maitre d served them appetizers. Looking at the small bowl, Yasmina was shocked to find a bowl full of marijuana inside.

"Did you see what the lady left on the table?" she looked at Scorcher.

"No worry, mon, it's alright," he replied as he started twisting a joint up.

Me'yard was the only restaurant on the island of its kind. Weed was an aphrodisiac served in the place, and people were free to smoke it without any qualms. The custom was adopted from Amsterdam, and it attracted prestigious clientele from all across the island. It took a lot of political influence to make it a success, but with drugs, power and money was influence enough. There was a hundred dollar cover charge, and you had to have connections to enter the restaurant. Scorcher's came in the form of Shotty Dread.

That night as they conversed and smoked ganja, they also heard some of the best reggae bands play live. Dub Mystic, Truth & Rights, Shaka Demus and Pliers, and a host of others helped in relaxing them so they could enjoy the night. After achieving his first surprise, Scorcher sought out the second one. It was nine o'clock and the ferry was about to leave. Negril, Jamaica was an hour and a half by boat ride so they had to hurry. Earlier in the week, Scorcher had purchased the tickets. He wanted to show Yasmina the good side of life in Jamaica. Their destination was to the casinos located on the infamous Merrils Beach, a Jamaican version of Atlantic City.

While sailing the slightly choppy waters of the ocean, Yasmina relaxed in the comfort of Scorcher's arms. As they talked, she reeled in the time she was having. Never in her wildest dream did she think that she'd be able to sit inside a public restaurant and smoke as much weed as she could. Then to have live reggae bands play for them, only up the potency of the weed. This was something truly out of the movies, and she couldn't wait to tell Selena.

The Blackjack Tables were crowded, but when Scorcher placed the chips worth five-thousand dollars on it, a spot was immediately cleared.

"Gwan' on, try your luck!" he gently placed her in front of the table. Yasmina couldn't believe what she was hearing. This guy just told her to play until she loses it all. This was truly unbelievable. Where she was from, coming across five grand was like hitting the lottery. Every now and then, her and Selena would run across a sucker for a couple a hundred bucks, but not five grand. Shit, not even a thousand, she thought as she watched the dealer shuffle the cards. As her cards were turned, a bunch of awes emitted from the crowd of spectators. This happened for three straight hands. But on the fourth hand, she struck some luck. Playing a thousand dollars a hand was beginning to dwindle her stack tremendously at first, but when she caught her luck, the stack started to rise. Now, all you heard was ooh, oh, and every now and then, a loud round of applause. When it was all said and done, she walked out the casino with $15,000.

"Here's your five grand," she held the money out to Scorcher.

"No shawty, you take that. You won it, so you keep it all." He reached over and kissed her passionately. "Shawty, mi dig your style, and mi like you a lot, but there's some tings' you don' know 'bout me. Mi want to know you on a more personal level, but mi live a dangerous life."

Yasmina stared deeply into his eyes as he spoke. To hear him pour his heart out, pained her, but there was also a new found respect. She could almost understand why he didn't sleep with her. But little did he know, she liked him very much, and wanted to be a part of his life despite the danger. It's what a woman is willing to put up with if she loves a man, she thought to herself.

"Scorcher, I liked you from the first time I laid eyes on you. It was something different about you that attracted me to you. You're very respectful, and you always carry yourself like a gentleman. That's hard to find these days. I also would like to pursue a relationship with you, but we're six hundred miles apart. How would that work? I mean, I can live with the danger because life in itself is dangerous. You never know when it's your time. But I know I don't want to leave without experiencing love for the first time. And I want it to be with you."

Immediately after the words left her mouth, he grabbed her, embracing her with a long kiss. So engulfed into the moment, they were not aware of the spectators who had gathered around, and were cheering "that's the girl who won all that money." That night, the two of them officially became an item.

There was one more surprise for Yasmina, and Scorcher figured since it was late, the timing would be perfect. He'd felt bad the past couple of days for not making any moves on her, but the timing wasn't right. He wanted the moment to be special, something they could savor. The Triple-X Club was a Vegas style strip club where both men and women went. The attractions were suited for both, and not knowing if she'd like it, he took his chance. He also could tell there was a freaky side to her. When he met her at spring bling, she was wearing one of the sexiest outfits at the beach. Her oiled legs glistened every time the sun reflected on her, and it turned him on. Not to mention, her manicured toes looked good enough to suck on. It was just something about her that captivated his attention, and piqued his curiosity.

After entering the club, the first thing they noticed were women dancing on stage. This didn't faze her in the least. The women on stage didn't have anything on her, plus she did this back at school. Taking her seat, this made her think of Scorcher in another light. The typical baller, he figured this would arouse her to a point where she would want to have sex, wrong! She thought before fully taking the seat.

Hearing him tell the waitress to send a bottle of Dom Perignon to the back, she wondered what was going on. "Does he have a V.I.P. Room back there somewhere? What's up this nigga's sleeves? I hope he don't think he's getting some nookie in this hole in the wall club." Rounding the corner, she entered into an entirely different world. The club had somehow expanded by sixty feet, and through glass windows, she would see women sexing men and women sexing women. Her juices started to flow. As the strobe lights turned, creating images in the dimly lit room, Yasmina started getting hotter. Accepting her drink from Scorcher, the slightest touch of his hand caused her to have a hot flash. When he pushed a button on the wall, a red-neon light came on – enclosing them in a room by themselves. Soft music started playing and the glass window slowly came into view. What she saw blew her mind. Two women were in the midst of sexing each other. Every time one would nibble on the other nipple, Yasmina would squeeze her legs together. She couldn't concentrate. Never in her life did she think she'd ever be turned on by watching two women. Back at U of M, her and Selena performed strip shows together, but they'd never thought of paying attention to each other's body. It was strictly a hustle.

The ladies writhed together as they both pleasured each other. Out the corner of her eye, she could see the long imprint of Scorcher's dick in his sweat suit. She longed for him to touch her. When one lady started eating the other, it drove her to her wits end. She couldn't take it anymore. Reaching over and grabbing Scorcher's penis, she removed it from inside his velour sweats. Massaging it, she was amazed at its thickness. Rubbing her fingertip across the tip cause him to jerk and tremble from the pleasure. Seconds later, she was riding him.

With her feet sitting atop his shoulders, she rode him and cried out in ecstasy as he pumped deep inside her, using circular motions. Their actions were so noticeable, the women behind the glass stopped to watch them go at it. This spurred all of them on to have more aggressive sex while watching each other perform. When the action reached it's highest, both Yasmina and Scorcher cried out as they reached orgasm. Sweat started dripping off their bodies in heaps.

The ferry ride back to Kingston was a blissful one for Yasmina. She won $15,000 at the casinos, smoked weed while a band played in a restaurant, and finally had sex with Scorcher, while others looked on. And it was good. Sitting in his arms as morning was breeding through the clouds, she rested her eyes as she lay on his chest. The breeze was doing wonders on the ocean, and she didn't want this spectacular morning to end.

Yasmina knew she was in love. She'd never felt this way before about anyone, and the fact that she had only one more day left in Kingston, hit her hard. Scorcher wanted to take her shopping. However, there was a tradition on the island that everyone followed, and it would be included in today's events. Scorcher took her to every fashion boutique in Wildman Square. He bought her things that only long money could buy. In Miami, a couple hundred dollars could buy you a nice outfit on Ocean drive; thousands could buy you a wardrobe. The boutiques were the same as the ones in Miami or on Rodeo Drive. By the end of the day, she purchased Gucci, Prada, Burberry, Coach, Dior, Channel, and Dolce Gabana. Total cost, $15,000. Her sophomore year, she knew she'd be the shit, and this wasn't the fifteen grand she'd won playing Black Jack.

The tradition on the island took place every Saturday night. The islanders loved chicken, so a curry chicken soup was the ideal meal celebrated. There was a catch to it, though. The soup consisted of a chicken foot, simmered with a broth. Many Jamaicans believed that the chicken foot possessed special powers, sort of like a good-luck charm. After the festive meal, and another night of great sex, the two lay cuddled in the bed. She woke up early Sunday morning and noticed that she was alone once again. Searching the bathroom, she couldn't find him there. This time she was sure he'd slept with her, his scent was all over the bed. Something caught her eye as she made it back to the bed. Walking over to the dresser, she found a small box with a red ribbon wrapped around it.

While Yasmina soundly slept, he had gotten up early and packed her bags in the Mercedes. Her flight was leaving at two and he wanted to make sure they had enough time in between. Earlier in the week, he'd ventured to a jewelry shop and had a special gift made for her. The delivery man delivered it bright and early in the morning while she slept. When he walked in the room, she jumped in his arms, hugging him and kissing him.

"Oh my gosh, this is beautiful!" She held the diamond tennis Bracelet with her initials engraved in it.

"You Like?" he smiled and asked.

Placing another kiss on his lips, she said, "I love it. It's the most beautiful thing I've ever seen." She kissed him again, stink breath and all.

Her happiness was followed with a sad afterthought. She was leaving within a couple of hours. It would be bye-bye Scorcher, and back to Miami. This was the one day she didn't want to walk through Manley International Airport in Kingston.

```
```````````````````````
```

**Four years later**

As Delta Flight #1598 came to a stop at LAX – Airport in Los Angeles, her adrenaline kicked in to a higher notch. Ever since September 11, 2001 happened, every airport across the nation went to the extremes of beefing up security. Making it through any airport then was like a prisoner being searched. All your dignity was thrown out the window. Luggage was being dumped onto tables if they suspected you in the least bit, and people were cordoned off into different groups where identification and passports were scrutinized to the
```

fullest. It was total chaos, and Yasmina once again was trying to make her way through, undetected.

The slightly large Coach bag, which was used as a pocket book by Yasmina, slid on the conveyor belt as it tried making its way through the checkpoint. Hearing the beep, she knew trouble was coming next. From amidst the crowd of hundreds who milled around aimlessly in the crowded airport, Yasmina could very well make out the armed National Guards members who carried the semi-automatic machine guns and pistols, which were now pointed in her direction. Panicking, the onlookers screamed and peered their heads to see what the ruckus was about, while Yasmina remained ingrained and calm. She expected this.

The interrogation room was basically a janitor's closet converted into a room, minus the chemicals. By the look of things, Yasmina knew this was going to be an all day matter. Opting to fly, she didn't feel like riding for seven days aboard the cruise ship. She'd been doing it too much lately, and the money she was carrying was too much to be hauling around aboard a ship. Sitting in the hard-steel chair, she didn't know how long she could take the three white men who smoked the smelly cigars and talk down on her like they were back in slavery days.

"Mrs. Powell," the chubby one said, "What on earth are you doing with $50, 000 dollars in the airport? We already know its drug money, it's just a matter of time before we find your other bags." The cigar dangled out of his mouth as he talked.

"What are you saying," Yasmina venomously spat back, "a Black woman can't have that type of money these days without people thinking it came from drugs?" Not liking the tone of this young black woman, who was trying to sound too educated, the chubby guy responded, but this time the smile on his face was gone, "No you can't, missy. For all we know, you're probably funding the terrorist that are trying to destroy the infrastructure of our beautiful country. That money's in violation of the Homeland security Act, and we'll have to confiscate that bag of yours," he sarcastically said. "I think the I.R.S. would love this."

While the one guy tried his best to humiliate Yasmina, his two cohorts laughed and cheered him on. They were succeeding in embarrassing the young Black female, plus this was one more arrest to add to their resumes.

"I think not!" she sharply replied when they finished their laughing spiel. "You, the I.R.S., or the Federal Government won't be confiscating a damn thing."

Hearing the tone of her voice, all three guys faces turned red, and ashes fell to the table as the chubby guy started to protest. Only to be cut short by her interruption.

"If you would've asked if I had paperwork for the money and not try to accuse me of funding terrorist and dealing drugs, this situation would've been cleared up a long time ago." She told them where to find the papers in her purse. She also knew that they didn't find anything else, or she'd be headed to the county jail already. With a smirk on her face, she said, "Can I please be excused now, or do I need to contact my lawyer, Sir?"

Looking in the direction of each other, the three white guys were furious. They just knew they'd caught someone red-handed, and a Black person, too. After reading the voucher word for word, she was told to leave. Luckily the date was valid. It allowed her to carry the money with the intent of purchasing items deemed necessary to their Import/Export Business. Something Scorcher had been doing the entire time.

40

Previous to the altercation she'd had in LAX, she had just flown from Miami. It was another pick-up she had made. Now, arriving to the baggage claim are, she sighed deeply seeing the Louis Vuitton Suitcase sitting on the conveyor belt. Luckily she followed Scorcher's advice and put an alias on it. With this stroke of genius, she managed to make it through one of the toughest checkpoints since Homeland Security started, with $2.5 million dollars. Security wasn't as tight as they think, she thought as she walked out the door.

Since her graduation from University of Miami, life has been good for Yasmina. She graduated with honors and the world was hers to conquer. Prestigious companies such as Merrill Lynch, Viacom, and Turner Networks were a few that sought her expertise. On the other end, Selena followed closely in her footsteps. After graduating, she pursued law. First, she went to a small firm and did intern work, but she knew her skills could be awarded more. Cochran and Cochran Associates hired her to be a Criminal Lawyer. The idea of becoming a partner in a couple of years was a possibility to her. After they went their separate ways, the two seldom saw each other, but constantly kept in touch via phone. Before fully accepting the role as a career woman, Yasmina wanted to spend a couple of months in Kingston with Scorcher. She had good intentions, and after the break was over, she'd be a full-fledged working woman, at least that's what she told her Grandmother. It didn't happen.

Her vacation was starting aboard the carnival cruise ship. Murray had given her one bag and it was for Scorcher. She asked no questions or snooped in the bag. She was ready for her journey. She was just happy to be going on her two month vacation, and spending time with her man.

After making it to the Mansion, Scorcher took her into the bedroom. He was happy that she came, but he was also happy about something else. As she lay back on the bed in anticipation of him diving into her and showing how much he missed her, he did the unthinkable. Opening the bag, he removed a couple pieces of clothing then dumped what was left of the contents atop Yasmina. Seeing the stacks of crisp money all over her and the bed, she was dumbfounded. After hearing Scorcher tell her that she'd just brought back a million dollars, it changed her life forever. She never made it to any of those prestigious companies that wanted her skills.

5

"PAPER CHASIN"

Trips to Miami, Chicago, New York, and California were a regular thing for Yasmina. Although the Importing/Exporting Business was one aspect of the business, there was another side of it. She became the liaison for Scorcher's drug empire. This consisted of collecting and routing money from the different connects that Scorcher held in each of the cities. She held meetings when necessary, and relayed information about the various pick-up and drop-off spots. Los Angeles was always the last spot hit. From there, the money would be transferred to an anonymous cargo ship, which Scorcher paid the Captain handsomely-then it would be shipped to Kingston. The pier was San Pedro.

One day after having a sit down with Jaheim, Yasmina was dropped off at the pier. She was always there when the money was stashed aboard the ship. This was a precautionary measure Scorcher drilled into her head. Thinking back to the meeting she had with Jaheim earlier, her instincts told her something wasn't right. Normally when conducting business, he'd acknowledge her presence by speaking, and it wouldn't go any further. But for some reason or another, he kept inquiring about Scorcher's money, drugs, and whereabouts. This made her angry so she cut the conversation short.

Scorcher met Jaheim back in the summer of 1996. He was trying to promote Hip Hop and R&B Shows, and landed a plug out in Cali. Headlining the Show was

Tupac Shakur, and at that time, the West was taking the East Coast by storm. Though there was a bitter rival ensuing, Biggie Smalls, Nas, Mobb Deep, and various other artists from the east were on the roster. It was a way for him to clean some of his dirty money.

Weeks before the show began, Scorcher was approached by a guy that worked security for other shows that came through L.A. Jaheim mentioned that he had a close source who informed him that the acts from the Death Row Camp were going to be secured by real street gangsters – Crips and Bloods. Knowing how deep the beef went with the East and West Coast, he informed Scorcher that he knew a lot of dependable guys who would act as security for his East Coast Artists. The night of the show went successful. Little skirmishes here and there, but nothing major. Having proven well, Scorcher paid Jaheim and his staff well. Since that one night, he'd been receiving a hundred kilos of cocaine, every two months, like clockwork.

"I'm glad to be back home, Yasmina said as she hugged Scorcher, "this trip was more stressful than the others."

"What's wrong, baby?"

Explaining the long drawn out scenario that happened at LAX had Scorcher steaming. He thought someone probably had tipped security off about her coming through the airport. He'd been hearing a lot of things. Drying himself off, he walked beside the Olympic Size Pool and cursed himself. He knew she should've taken the cruise ship, but she didn't want to listen. Now the information he'd been hearing about Jaheim plagued his mind.

"Shawty, you alright?" he gave her a reassuring hug. He knew he couldn't let her go through LAX again, it was too dangerous. Another plan had to be implemented.

"I'm ai'ight, but you need to check your boy, Jaheim." A serious gaze came across her face. "That muthafucka kept asking me all kinds of questions about you. Like, when's the next shipment, where are we meeting, how many keys, and am I gonna count the money there. Oh yeah, he asked were you still in Kingston. That's when I left."

Hearing these words, basically confirmed Scorcher's intuitions. Slamming his fist on the table caused his drink to spill over. Murray told him that a reliable source said Jaheim was busted with a hundred keys. He knew what Jaheim was trying to do. He was trying to get Yasmina to say something incriminating. Explaining everything to her, he told her to lay low. He couldn't dare risk her going to jail, he loved her too much. Yasmina wasn't going to take this lying down. She was persistent about continuing regardless of what Jaheim was trying to do. But in reality, she was starting to become addicted to the money. Thoughts about doing her own thing crossed her mind too many times.

"Selena speaking, may I ask who's calling?"

"Damn bitch, you gotta act all professional and shit. You ain't on the job, relax," Yasmina burst out laughing in her ear on the phone.
It had been a while since Yasmina talked to Selena, and she was excited at hearing her voice.

"Hi Yas," Selena screamed into the phone. "How are you? How's Jamaica and Mr. Luva-Luva man treating you?"

"Everything's good."

"Girl, I thought you were one of my clients calling. You know I have to put the professional lingo down." Selena chuckled.

"Well brace yourself, 'cause I have some good news for you sista girl," Yasmina said.

Screaming, Selena asked, "Are you pregnant? I knew it, I just knew it girl. That mandingo brotha done put that thang on you and knocked you up. That's why your ass couldn't wait to g….."

"Slow down, girl," Yasmina interrupted in the middle of Selena's ranting and raving. "Damn! I see you haven't changed one bit. I bet you won't lose one single case with that mouthpiece of yours." She laughed. "Nah, but seriously, I need you to listen to me. No I'm not pregnant and no I'm not getting married. I'm coming home tomorrow and I n….."

"That nigga didn't hit you, did he?" she cut Yasmina off. "I don't wanna have to come to Jamaica and kill his ass."

"No it's not that, if you'll listen. I need you to pick me up from the airport tomorrow."

"Okay, but what did you have to tell me that was so important?" asked Selena.

"You'll just have to wait until you pick me up," answered Yasmina.

After hanging the phone up, Yasmina felt good. It would be the first time in months since she'd seen her friend, and there was a lot of catching up to do. During their Junior and Senior years of college, a lot of memorable moments were created. They partied and traveled everywhere together. If it wasn't on an all expense paid trip to Jamaica by Scorcher and Murray, it was to New York, Selena's home, in the Bronx.

46

When she first moved to Miami, Yasmina thought that it was the epitome of all cities. Huge skyscrapers covered the city and it was a melting pot for citizens of all races. However, after coming to New York, the city with eight million stories, her view changed. The skyscrapers were huge, almost reaching the clouds. The vast amount of people that walked the streets everyday made her think of Wall Street. But these were normal streets like Time Square in Manhattan, Grand Concourse in the Bronx, or Lenox Avenue in Harlem. One thing about New Yorkers, they move fast, and have a million and one thing to get into.

Again, they would shop the designer stores, but they were located in the huge Macy's Shopping Mall in Manhattan. Their men kept their pockets fat, so spending wasn't a problem. Back in school, this caused a whole lot of envy. To them, they were above the status of baller chicks, and therefore the name PLATINUM CHICKS came to life. This was more than a title, it was their creed. Expensive clothes, best champagne that money can buy, and five-star hotels, it was the life, and no ordinary Jane could use a title as such, because the ordinary Jane's didn't have men like Scorcher and Murray in their corners.

One night while they were at Selena's Mom's house, they decided to go hang out. All of Selena's friends kept telling her about JIMMYS, the hot spot located in the Bronx. So that night, she figured her and Yasmina would see what all the hype was about. After entering the sports club, they both received stares. Some were welcoming and others were menacing. Yasmina, having just left Macy's earlier that day, wore a candy red-denim Pelle Pelle pantsuit, with the Manolo Timbs to match. Selena, wore a denim Prada Bodysuit with her

Manolo's matching also. Once again, they were the eye candy that stood out amongst the women.

The first eye that was caught was Fat Joe's. He sat at a table surrounded by three women, one Dominican, a Boricua mommy and a Sista. He was doing it Big Willie Style. To see this, Yasmina became amazed. She couldn't believe the lengths some women went to be seen with a baller. Each of the girls catered to his every need. One of them even went as far as wiping his mouth after he ate. To her, this was something definitely out of the videos, she thought to herself. Not the one to hate, she figured they had to be some all right baller catchers, just not on the level as herself and Selena.

After they were led to their prospective tables, they were about to take their seats until Yasmina noticed two females walking in their direction, and they weren't waitresses. Going on the defensive, Yasmina balled her fist and discreetly whispered to Selena, who was unaware of it.

Yasmina learned the laws of the street at an early age. She was one to always be prepared for whatever, because things could happen at the drop of a dime, especially with jealous females. The two women finally made it over to the table, and the looks across their faces weren't to be trusted. Out of nowhere, a silver bucket that held a chilled bottle of Dom Perignon and two wine flutes were handed to them. Compliments of DMX, who stood by the bar holding a bottle of Hennessey V.S.O.P up, in a speaking gesture.

As the music cranked, they talked about the who's who that graced the inside of the club. Yasmina admitted that JIMMYS was running a race with the Club Level.

"You think he remembers us from the V.I.P in Club Level?" Selena asked.

"I don't know, he's probably trying to pull a stunt like Fat Joe and show everyone in here that he can have two drop-dead gorgeous bitches like us by his side also. One bottle of Dom Perignon ain't gon' do the job, though."
Yasmina jokingly laughed.

While they chatted, they were interrupted as DMX gave Yasmina a message. This confirmed for certain that he knew very well who they were. The message was to Scorcher. For a minute she felt stupid. Here she was, dating a guy that was fine, and gave her every and anything she needed, and she was making jokes about flirting with a friend of his.

"Girl, whatchu' thinking 'bout so hard?" Selena nudged her on the shoulder, breaking her out her stupor.

"I'm thinking about my man," she lied, but sort of was telling the truth.

"Damn!" exclaimed Yasmina. "I see that being a lawyer is treating you good. Look at 'chu, pushing the new BMW and shit."

"Hey, I wanna experience the good life too. And that's Criminal Lawyer, while you're at it." She smiled as she added emphasis on her words.
After the long ride from the airport, they finally made it back to Selena's condo. The thought of the surprise burned Selena up, and she was anxious to find out what it was. While eating, the two chatted about old times. This is when Yasmina let her in on the surprise. Not to say she was surprised, Selena was shocked. She couldn't believe that Yasmina was giving up the good job offers to move back to Jamaica.

"What's Mrs. Rosa going to say? Have you mentioned it to her yet?" asked Selena.

Yasmina didn't have an answer for that one. As far as her grandmother knew, she was coming back home for good, and starting her career. Yasmina feared this day. She already knew how her grandmother felt about Scorcher, and it wasn't good. Although she didn't know he was a drug dealer, there was something about him she couldn't quite place a finger on it. When Yasmina introduced him, she tried then to tell her about her gut feeling about him, but she wouldn't listen. Yasmina worshipped the ground Scorcher walked on.

"I still hadn't figured that one out," Yasmina answered sounding sad, "but one thing's for sure, she's not going to like it."

As far as Selena knew, Yasmina was going to work as a Marketing Analyst for some company in Kingston. This was good news for her because she didn't want her best friend to throw away her career because she was in love. Even Selena knew very well about how Scorcher made his living, but she didn't knock him. She only hoped that Yasmina would be smart enough not to partake in it. This conversation made her think to their days in college. It was their senior year, and Scorcher flew into town a couple of days before graduation. As the four got together, they didn't know of the big plans he and Murray had in store for them. Blindfolded, and riding somewhere in the huge Expedition Murray purchased weeks earlier, Selena and Yasmina sat side by side, not knowing what was about to happen. Coming to a stop, the blindfolds were lifted, and the only thing that could be heard were screams. It took a minute for their eyes to adjust, but seeing the matching Infiniti J-30s with red-ribbons tied around them, they couldn't help but scream. It was a graduation present.

That night, they went to Club Level and were spoiled by Scorcher and Murray. Sometime in the midst of partying, Murray and Scorcher disappeared. It was something they'd seen in the club and told the girls that they'd be back shortly. Well shortly was taking too long. While Yasmina and Selena sat in the V.I.P. sipping on their bubbly, they couldn't quite make themselves comfortable. Something was going on and they both could feel the vibes. Nervous and agitated every time the door opened, Yasmina would get up to peer into the crowd. The only thing that slightly calmed her nerves was listening to Lil Jon rip the mic and keeping the crowd hype.

Being in Club Level was sort of status symbol for them. The local ballers rather go to some club where they had to wear a bulletproof vest. However, being with Scorcher, she didn't have to think about things like that. There was no need. Scorcher and Murray really defined what supreme ballers were, and for them to be gone for thirty minutes, had the girls worried. As anticipation got the best of her, she bolted for the door.

"Where in the hell are you going?" asked Selena.

"Something ain't right; Scorcher and Murray are up to something." She bounced back from one foot to the other.

As Yasmina stepped out the door, she walked straight into Scorcher. He was making his way up the steps.

"Shawty, where are you going?" He yelled over the music.

"I was coming to look for you, you had me worried. It's been over thirty minutes," Yasmina said in a worried tone.

51

"Everything's alright. Mi thought mi saw an old business partner, that's all."

After making it back into the V.I.P, Yasmina could sense that everything wasn't okay. Scorcher had this weird look on his face and Murray was too quiet. He also kept looking through the glass window. Not pressing the issue, they left the club. Making it outside was chaotic. People were acting frantic, police cars lined the streets, and an ambulance was tending to someone. As Yasmina tried making her way closer to see what all the drama was about, she was stunned as she felt herself jerk back.

"Muthafucka, who you pullin' on like that. I ain't one of your bitches you can just jerk around." She shot venom at Scorcher. She was already upset. She thought he had gone to see another female in the club while they were left sitting in V.I.P..

"Just keep it moving. This doesn't have anyting' to do with us," he replied, not acknowledging anything she was saying.

"What do you mean-with us?" she retorted sarcastically.

Yasmina's voice kept getting louder and people were beginning to stare. This really began to irritate Scorcher. Too much attention isn't what he needed right now. Noticing the menacing gaze in his eyes, she closed her mouth and didn't utter another word. The entire trip to the hotel was in silence. After they made it to the room, Scorcher went directly to the phone.

"Yeah, it's me. Mi talk to you tomorrow, alright, peace."

The short-choppy conversation had Yasmina puzzled. She didn't know what to think. 'Was this fool talking to some bitch right in front of her face or what?' she thought to herself as she fumed while sitting on the bed.

Trying to avoid a fight, she turned the T.V. on. She knew if she sat in the midst of his presence too long, a brawl would ensue.

Channel 4 News was the first thing to appear on the screen. Already angry, she just needed something to fill the air other than quietness, so she didn't bother changing the channel. Barely listening, but apt enough to hear Club Level mentioned, she directed all her attention to what was being said. In the background, reporters were running a story about a body found buried in a trash heap, shot twice in the head. Her face registered shock, and the next thing she did was run into the bathroom. That's when she got the surprise of her life. Scorcher stood over the sink rinsing what appeared to be spatters of blood out of the IceBerg T-Shirt he'd worn to the club.

"Hey-hey come back here!" he yelled seeing her dash out of the bathroom.

Putting two and two together, Yasmina knew her intuitions were right. There was something going on and it spelled trouble. The way Scorcher and Murray acted was different. Thinking back to the club, she now understood why he wore the sweater over the white T-shirt.

"I knew you were acting strange when I stopped to see what was going on outside the club." She was clearly upset now.

"Shawty, mi apologize 'bout grabbing you, but someting' went down tonight and mi didn't wan' hang around." He was on bending knees looking up to her as she sat on the bed.

Listening to him explain what happened, Yasmina sat speechless. She loved him and thought their relationship was built on trust. For him to keep what happened from her, wasn't not trust. How could he jeopardize her safety and not inform her? The thought kept coming. She needed to know any and everything so she'd be able to provide an alibi. That's what people in love do.

After calming down, she sat back on the pillow. How could someone who owed another person $200,000 dollars, blatantly disrespect the person it's owed to? This cost that guy his life tonight, and Yasmina learned a valuable lesson. The game is real and it can be life or death..

6

"INGENIOUS"

The real reason for Yasmina coming back to Miami wasn't the reasons she'd told Selena and her grandmother about. She'd come back to put a team together, a team that would be known as the PLATINUM CHICKS. Over the years, her and Selena had grown apart, and their careers kept them from doing big things together. Although they would remain friends, life had to go on, and Yasmina had a big future ahead of her.

Though she'd been picking and delivering money for Scorcher, she was beginning to see that more money could be made by dealing the stuff. Her finances were straight, but all her life, she never had to depend on anyone to give her money or take care of herself. She wanted her own. Running the idea to Scorcher didn't get taken too well. He felt like she should be happy with what he was giving her. Her persistence overshadowed anything he tried to say. She wanted to make her mark in the game, and would stop at nothing to achieve this.

After relaying her strategy to him, she told him about the crew she intended on bringing in. Getting in touch with Stacey, Damita, and Latoya wasn't going to be easy, but she had an idea where they were. Yasmina met the girls when she was fifteen years old while living in Carol City. Her Grandmother always went to Liberty City to eat at a Jamaican Soul-Food Eatery on the weekends. This particular weekend, Yasmina finished eating early. Like clockwork, every Saturday for as long

55

as she could remember, she would see these same three girls outside jumping Double-Dutch. After finishing her food early, she decided to saunter across the street and watch. She really wanted to join in on the session but was skeptical. She kept getting mean stares. One of the girls, a huge brown-skinned full figured girl, always stared daggers at her, and this made her very reluctant in approaching. Deciding to head back to the restaurant, she heard someone yell out to her.

"Hey girl, com 'ere. Whatcho' name is?" she had a deep Florida accent.

"Yasmina," she nervously answered.

"You're not from around here, are ya?" asked the huge girl.

"No, I'm from Jamaica." Her accent was noticeable then.

"Hi, I'm Damita," another girl walked up introducing herself. "This is Stacey and Latoya."

From that day on, and every Saturday, she hung with her new friends. She started exploring new neighborhoods and meeting different guys. It was with her new friends that Yasmina experienced her first blunt, and the idiom "chasing ballers" was brought into action. And everyday, one of them talked about becoming rich and marrying a baller. Yasmina was well on her way.

After getting her license a few years later, Yasmina went to Liberty City almost every night of the week. She would hop into her grandmother's old-Buick Celebrity and ride back and forth from Carol City to Liberty City. The car was basically riding on fumes. A couple weeks before her high school graduation, she started dating a small time dealer named Jaleel. She was introduced to him by Damita after scraping up enough money to purchase a bag of weed from him. Jaleel had all the chicks on his jock. His light grey eyes and curly hair attracted Yasmina the moment she'd laid eyes on him. Since he was making a little bit of noise in their eyes, it impressed them. He was a baller. Back in the 90's, anyone slinging a little bit of dope was considered a baller to the young females, as long as they were able to keep you high and pay for dinner at Mickey D's, it was all good.

One night as the two sat in Olinda Park smoking weed, the unknown happened. Yasmina sat atop the trunk of the car, wearing a short mini-skirt while Jaleel stood between her legs. She was a virgin at the time but she didn't mind him fondling her. She was determined to let him be the first. As the action continued, she puffed on the blunt completely unaware of any and everything around her. Jaleel had specifically told her to watch for slow moving cars approaching. A lot of drive-by shootings were happening and the police cruised the place all the time. While engaged in their teenage lusting, the lights of an oncoming car slowly approached. Aware of what was happening, Jaleel slowly began to stop what he was doing and found his gun. Yasmina, so engulfed in the moment, didn't notice anything going on as she sat with her eyes closed. Finally realizing the car was only a few feet away, it was too late.

"Freeze!" came the voice of the police officer. "Hands up and face the car," the deep voice boomed.

Shocked and high from the marijuana, Yasmina sat still. Her panties halfway down her legs, and the blunt still burning in her hand. How was she going to explain this to her grandmother? she thought to herself as tears welled up in her eyes. Before she could collect her thoughts, Jaleel bolted for the trail that led through the woods. It was pitch black and this freaked Yasmina out.

The officers left in pursuit as she sat in the same position. For a moment, she wondered why Jaleel ran. Why the cops drew their guns at him and why they didn't put her in the squad car?

Hearing the loud blast told her everything she'd questioned herself about. Seeing the cops dive for cover and Jaleel letting off round after round, panic and fear caused her to urinate on herself. Crying and nervous, she managed to insert the key into the ignition while trembling terribly. Driving out of the park, she didn't look back or stop until she pulled into her grandmother's yard. The next day she made up an excuse to stay home. Her nerves were too shot. Around noon, she received a phone call.

"Girl, did you hear what happened to Jaleel last night?" asked Damita.

"Did I, I was with that crazy muthafucka when he shot at the cops."

"What, for real?" exclaimed Damita in disbelief.

"Damita, I swear, one minute we were getting high and the next, this fool just started blasting at them. It was crazy," Yasmina relayed in disbelief herself.

"Are you alright?"

"I am now. But last night I was a nervous wreck. I even pissed on myself. Look, when you see that fool again, you tell him to stay the hell away from me."

"Well, I don't think you'll have to worry about that anymore. That fool killed one of the cops and got shot in the process. It was all over the news. His ass is going to prison for a long time. And peep this, they said that he was wanted for another murder. Some drug dealer he'd killed a couple of months ago."

Hearing this, Yasmina couldn't say anymore. Finding out Jaleel murdered someone in the Groves bothered her. She'd been dating this fool for a month and didn't know he was a psycho. She cursed herself for being so stupid.

After moving to college, it was the last time she'd seen or heard from her old friends. Now that she was back in Miami, Yasmina set forth with her intended plan to find Damita, Latoya and Stacey.

"Grandma, you have this place looking nice, "Yasmina complimented, seeing that the old house held a lot of new furniture.

"Well, you know mi do what mi can, it's the only home mi have."

"Why don't you let me move you out this old house? We can find you something better out in Coconut Groves. This neighborhood is too dangerous. I know the money I send you is more than enough to cover your bills," said Yasmina.

"Mina, you know dis has been mi home for decades, and it's yours also. Mi will not leave. Mi had many great years in this house."

After seeing that she wasn't going to persuade her grandmother into moving, Yasmina joined her for dinner. It was a long time since she had homemade Ox-tails, and her grandmother still knew how to make her favorite meal,

Rosa left Kingston back in the 60's. It was the beginning of some vicious fighting over Independence, and she feared not making it to a better life because of all the bloodshed. There were many heated discussions brewing between both political parties, the Jamaican Labor Party and the Peoples National Party. And with them planning to overthrow the government, she figured it was time to leave. Back then, the House of Representatives gladly issued guns to both parties; in hope that they'd kill each other.

Knowing that life was hard enough and times were changing, Rosa and Thomas saved every penny possible in hopes of fleeing to a better life. Miami would be this ideal place of freedom.

Scraping and scrounging, Yasmina's grandfather managed to save enough money to send Rosa to Miami. However, there was another problem, Yasmina's father Frank wouldn't be able to go along on the journey. There wasn't enough money. Feeling that someone had to be in Miami to set the foundation, he urged Rosa, practically begging her to board the ship that waited at the docks, promising her that as soon as he gathered the money, they'd be close behind.

No matter how degrading the circumstances were, the price of freedom was worth it. So Rosa suffered living in the cramp quarters of a supply room for twelve days. More than twenty people joined her on the long and horrible journey, but she survived. While telling Yasmina this story for the first time ever, tears crowded both their eyes. She continued by telling Yasmina that every week her and Thomas kept in touch by mail. This was in order to keep hope alive, because one day they planned to be together again. 1961 was fast approaching and he hadn't yet come up with the money. With the bloodshed increasing at an alarmingly rate, it was now or never.

At the time, Yasmina's father was a young child, but he was well aware of what was happening. One night as he and Thomas snuck into the mountains to a secret spot where they stashed every penny saved, trouble found them. They were cornered by two rebels. Being as silent as possible, they crept through the darkness in hopes of avoiding something like this, but couldn't. The two men brandishing machetes surrounded them, and fear gripped them. They were being forced to hand over all the money they possessed, and Thomas wasn't going for that. The money was their path to freedom, and he wasn't about to let anyone take that away. When one of the men grabbed Frank and put the sharp blade of the machete under his neck, Thomas snapped. Without hesitation, he leaped at the man, taking him by surprise. In the darkness, they tussled in the dirt and grass until Thomas got the better of the man. Wrestling the sharp knife away, he managed to slash the man across the throat, causing him to drown in his own blood. The other man, in rage and fear, charged after Thomas. In the quiet of the night you could hear two hard breathing shadows, and every now and then, sparks would briefly fly through the air at the heavy blades clinked together. Seconds later, a shrilling cry was heard, as the blade of a machete embedded itself into the gut of Thomas. One last swing decapitated the head from his body.

In tears and fear, Frank ran for his life. He finally made it back to his village. He stayed enclosed inside the small shanty home for days, hoping the man wouldn't come for him. After writing to Rosa, he explained the tragic news. At the time, she wasn't a legal citizen and couldn't risk going back to bury her husband. As fate would have it, that turned out to be the last time she saw her husband and son alive. Thinking about the many things that happened to her loved ones, she didn't understand why Yasmina wanted to go back to that place.

"I don't see why you wan' go back to dat place, Yasmina." Rosa held a worried look.

"Ah Mama, Kingston has changed greatly. I mean, it still has it's impoverished areas, but there's more business there now. I'm going to keep working at the new job I have, it pays me just as much as the companies here in the states are offering me. It's an American based Import/Export Consortium, and I'm head Marketing Analyst. The same thing I went to school for," Yasmina tried her best to lie.

"Who is this boy you're in love with? I hope it's not that boy you brought to my house when you were in college."

Yasmina was shocked hearing what her grandmother had said. Not once did she mention she was in love.

"Mama, that's not the reason I went back. I took the job because of the money."

"Young lady, you can fool a cat but you can't pull de' wool over my eyes. Mi wiseness goes beyond your years, remember that. Also, if tings don't work out with you and that boy, remember you always have a home right here," she smiled and opened her arms for a hug.

Since Yasmina went back to Jamaica, she made sure sent her grandmother $3000 dollars every month. Like clockwork, it would arrive at Western Union on the same date every month. She did this to make sure that all the bills were paid without a problem, and it showed that she was really working a job, at least she thought. After spending the day with her grandmother, she went to handle her business. To bring her plans together, she headed across town to Liberty City, Damita's domicile.

"What's up, girl? Damn, you looking good!" Damita stared Yasmina up and down.

"How have you been yourself?" asked Yasmina, looking around the one bedroom apartment that held five people.

"As you can see, I'm still at home with my Momma and her boyfriend. These are my two sons, Derek and Jamie." She rubbed their heads as they each held onto her legs.

After talking for awhile with her long time friend, Yasmina took Damita out for drinks. She wanted to feel Damita out before broaching the subject of making money, but Damita said the words she was looking to hear. She kept stressing her welfare situation and how much the government kept cutting her food stamps, and not having any money to do things for her kids. Just like many inner city males, Damita's kids' father was locked up in prison for murder, leaving her to be a single parent trying to raise two kids.

"You wanna make some money?" The question was simple.

"Girl, whatchu' talkin' about?" Damita sat not knowing where Yasmina was heading. "You went to college and all so I know you're doing good for yourself. I don't even have a High School Diploma. Ain't no..."

"Look, enough with feeling sorry for yourself. Do you wanna make some money or not?" she stared at Damita unwaveringly.

Running down everything to Damita, the look on her face showed she was down. Yasmina explained that she needed a thorough team of females and told her who she had in mind. She also stated the way they were going to be pushing big weight, so it was no time for games. An hour after meeting with all three girls, it was official. Yasmina had achieved what she set out to, and the PLATINUM CHICKS were formed this time as a crew.

7
"MONEY, MONEY, AND MORE MONEY"

"Latoya, if these niggas do as much as flinch wrong, you lay their asses out," Yasmina instructed Latoya as the deal went down.

"Ai'ight," Latoya shook her head in response as the Desert Eagle stood cocked and ready in her hand.

The PLATINUM CHICKS had been hitting certain parts of Miami hard the past few months. After getting the green light from Scorcher, Yasmina turned the heat up to full blast. They were certified Brick Layers.

To insure that she wasn't going into the game wearing a blindfold, Scorcher taught her every aspect of hustling. That included the rules of the game. In the first few weeks, she learned how to cut the coke and cook it. Next, she learned every aspect of weighing on triple beams, then the digital scale. From there, concealing the coke was the next lesson, and the teachings went on and on. The most important thing he wanted her to realize was, the game in itself was a very dangerous and sheisty one. If caught slipping, she could easily come up short on her cash, or for that matter, missing. There was no rules when it came to dealing drugs. At the end of her lesson, she did what every dealer across the nation did; she purchased a drug kit and guns.

Now that her crew were bona fide hustlers, they set out to get paid. Using the Import/Export Business as a front, Yasmina shipped her product into the Miami

Harbors. After unloading and transferring the work to a secure storage unit, she contacted the Platinum Chicks. While riding to meet their prospective clients, the words Scorcher said played over and over in her mind. "Don't trust anyone". With that in mind, Yasmina knew she couldn't mess up this first run, her reputation was on the line and being tested. Even though he said he'd take the loss if things didn't go right, she was determined to make it work. This would be her mark in the game.

While pulling up into the apartment complex, Yasmina could feel the tension overcoming her. Shrugging it off, her and Latoya continued up the flight of stairs until they made it to the door of the apartment. This is when a weird feeling overtook both of them. The complex had only one way to enter and one way to leave, and this didn't sit well with either of them. But they were there to handle business, so that's what they did. Getting her gun ready, Yasmina said to Latoya, "if we don't make it out alive, no one will." Deep down inside, she wished the guys would've met them. This felt like a set up. Why should she have to bring the coke? Shouldn't they meet me on my terms? I'm the one calling the shots. These thoughts played terribly on Yasmina's mind, but it was too late to turn back.

After entering the apartment, both tried to assess the joint. They wanted to know if someone was peeping out the extra bedroom, coming out the closet, or waiting behind the sofa to jack them for everything they had. This wasn't the case. The only people to occupy the small apartment were two men, a white man and a black man. They sat at a table where a triple beam scale sat positioned directly in front of them. As Latoya stood close by with the gun in hand, Yasmina handled business.

"You got the money?" her words were precise and to the point as she stared unblinkingly at the two men. "Here's your brick."

"Look, I don't play games when it comes down to this shit. As long as your money's correct, we both will be satisfied, now won't we." It wasn't a question, but a statement. "Don't make me have to come back because you short me."

When the transaction was complete, her and Latoya bounced out the apartment with a duffle bag full of money. After making it safely to the car, the two of them exhaled loudly. They were scared shitless. Latoya, whose only role was to be the muscle, received her two grand. It was a deal made between the two as they sat down and negotiated the first night Yasmina talked with them. Her deals were two-grand off of every deal made. And that meant that she had to always be ready to bust her gun, at any given moment.

As it were, things were going good. The customers were getting the best quality of coke (Peruvian flake) from Yasmina, their signature was known, and money started coming in by the case loads. Wanting to always be a step ahead, she advised her crew to spend some money and relocate their families. It wouldn't be wise to lay your head where you did your dirt.

"Damita, you and the girls come up to my room around 7:30 p.m., I'm at the Ritz Carlton on Ocean Drive, room 1403. Oh yeah, wear some fly shit 'cause we're going to celebrate tonight." She hung the phone up.

An hour later after Yasmina was dressed, there was a knock on the door. "What's up! Come on in." Yasmina was glad to see the girls had arrived. And they were dressed to impress. "I was waitin' on y'all hoes to come over so we could kick it on the town tonight," she smiled. Everything Yasmina did was about making money. Even going out on the town was an indirect way of getting paid. This was to procure more clientele.

"Damn, this room is the shit!" exclaimed Stacey. "I've never been in one this big, and it has a Jacuzzi in the middle of the floor."

Hearing this, Yasmina thought back to when her and Selena were in college. Almost every five star hotel that they had graced with Scorcher had a Jacuzzi in the center of the floor. This made her laugh to herself.

"I know this had to run you a good trip," replied Latoya.

"Try $4,000 dollars for a week." Yasmina smiled.

"4,000 dollars!" Damita blurted aloud. "Damn, you living like the stars do, girl."

"That's exactly the point I'm trying to show you all. You can be living like this also, as long as you keep it real with me. It's a lot of paper out there for us to get, and I intend on staking my claim while the getting is good." She lit a blunt of ganja that she saved for this occasion. "Now, are y'all down?"

"I'm down," Damita spoke first. "Yeah we're down, shit!" Stacey answered for her and Latoya.

"I'll finally be able to give my boys a life, thank you Yasmina." She walked over and hugged her.

That night, the Platinum Chicks pulled into the parking lot of the Rolex Club in a 2001 candy apple-red Escalade, sitting on chrome. They were impressed watching Yasmina whip the big truck in and out of traffic. Soon, they all knew they'd be able to floss a nice ride, because all of them had been saving their money. They were getting good prices on the coke.

67

After entering the club, they found a table close by the stage. From the moment they walked in the door, the first noticeable thing were the women, naked women dancing around as men tossed dollar bills at them. This was where Yasmina knew she could find the clientele she needed. Every baller liked to treat himself every now and again. Not wanting the girls to feel uncomfortable, she explained her reasons for bringing them. At first glance, anyone would've assumed they were a bunch of lesbians when they walked through the door. Why else would four nice looking females hangout at a male strip club?

Yasmina ordered and paid for a few rounds of drinks. She even issued out six hundred dollars worth of ones between the girls. Seeing the women do their thing on stage reminded Yasmina of her days back at U of M. Her and Selena would have made good strippers, but she had her eyes on the bigger prize, she thought of herself while sipping on a cocktail. While in her reverie, she was brought back to reality when she noticed a stripper coming to their table. As if on cue, Latoya whipped out twenty one- dollar bills and slid them into the girl's G-string. Adjusting her body, she sat splay legged as the girl began doing a lap dance for her. This tripped Yasmina out. The men in the club started applauding the girls because they were spending money and enjoying the erotic show just as much as they were. This prompted Yasmina and the rest of the girls to tip the dancer more. She knew it would draw attention from the ballers, and it worked. Not even a second after the dancer walked off, two guys came over and introduced themselves. The Platinum Chicks accepted their drink offers. "Ch-ching," Yasmina whispered to herself. She knew they'd just added two new prospects to their clientele. After leaving the club, they talked with the two guys for awhile in the parking lot. Info was exchanged and then they went their separate ways.

"Latoya, girl you freaked me out when you called that girl over to dance." Yasmina laughed while she drove.

"Oh, you think I did it for fun. Shit, I was trying to take that home with me tonight!" Latoya stated confidently. "That fat ass would've looked good in my bed. That's ai'ight though, I got those digits, she'll be hearing from me real soon."

Yasmina didn't know whether to take what Latoya said seriously or not. Everyone else started laughing. They knew she was crazy enough to do something like that. When they got to Yasmina's room, they talked about the fun they had, how good it felt to go out and enjoy spending money. As they conversed, Yasmina told them about the next shipment. They move twenty-five bricks in a month's time, and she'd be bringing more on the next go around. If there was anything to be said, she'd proven that this game was for her. It was time to expand their horizons, and that meant networking from state to state. North Carolina, make way, the Platinum Chicks were I-95 bound.

The flight to Jamaica seemed to take forever. Yasmina felt like kissing the ground when she finally made it back home. Walking into the Mansion, she was happy to see Scorcher. The month she'd been gone felt like two, but she had to make sure her business was tight. Being away so long made her realize just how much she loved him.

As she stood by the bed with her back turned, Scorcher walked up on her; wrapping his arms around her waist-kissing her on her neck. Being gone for so long also made her horny, and she wanted him bad, but business was first. Pushing him away, she reached for the silver briefcase. Opening it, she dumped the contents of more than $350,000 dollars onto the bed. She then looked at him and said, "you tink' my game is tight enough?"

Although Jaheim was making three times more than that for Scorcher, he knew that Yasmina was going to step up big time. Besides, Jaheim would be dealt with soon enough.

"Mi see you did your ting'." He passionately kissed her. "You know what, that's yours. Mi have to admit though, mi was really worried. You were taking so long to come back."

"I had to make sure everything ran smooth. I can honestly say that I have a team of down ass-bitches." She smiled.

"When you finish your next shipment, we're gwan to Ochos Rios for a couple weeks. Mi have something' mi want to show you." He climbed atop her and the pile of money, and began making love to her. This was a new beginning and probably a bad ending for both her and Scorcher.

8

"I-95 NORTH BOUND"

Damita phoned Yasmina the minute her and Latoya made it to the hotel in Winston-Salem. They made it with no problems, so that was enough for her and Stacey to follow suit. Immediately after hearing those words, they hit the highway, but Yasmina didn't feel as comfortable. When her plane arrived at MIA International, she couldn't believe what she was seeing. Stacey sat in the parking lot in a brand new 2001 Lexus 430, dipped in chrome.

The plan was for her to rent a mini-van like Damita and Latoya had done, but it was too late. Since Damita had family in Winston-Salem, Yasmina decided that it would be their next money spot. Her philosophy on hustling was, she couldn't be in one place too long. She learned that from Scorcher and Jaheim. Scorcher had gotten a little too personal with him, and that made it easier for Jaheim to turn on Scorcher when shit got hot. Being a fast learner, Yasmina knew she couldn't get too comfortable in one spot. Plus she heard it was a lot of money to be made there.

Every summer, Damita and her two sons would board the Greyhound Bus, and head to Winston-Salem. She had an aunt who lived there, and with nothing to do in Miami, she felt like getting away for a while. While hanging out with her cousins Tamika and Dalvin, she would see people hustling, making money on a regular. At the clubs, ballers would floss their rides and flash

71

money like it grew on trees. Even though he was small time, her cousin Dalvin hustled crack and weed, so Damita knew there was plenty money to be made, and that's when she told Yasmina.

After finding out how to get across town, Damita and Latoya drove the mini-van with the fifty bricks to a storage unit. They followed precise instructions to pack the work in three empty 27 inch T.V. boxes and left. On the way back to her aunt's house, they told Dalvin how things were going to go down. However, business wouldn't begin until Yasmina made it in, safely.

As Yasmina and Stacey drove up the highway, many thoughts went through Yasmina's mind as she sat in the passenger's seat. She couldn't believe the gall of Stacey. How could she drive this hot ass Lexus? This was definitely a no-no. Why would her stupid ass drive this flashy ass car knowing they were dirty? If they were caught with all the work that was in the trunk, they'd never see the outside again, as she watched for any signs of unmarked police cars.

Driving through Georgia and South Carolina, paranoia began to set in on Yasmina. She couldn't count on two hands how many unmarked Police Mustangs that sat hidden in the median. That didn't include seeing Stacey going over the speed limit. Oblivious to anything around her, Stacey bounced her head up and down as the crisp music banged in their ears. As she sped passed cars, she acted like two large Army Duffle bags of Cocaine wasn't sitting in the trunk. Every time an unmarked police car would bolt out of the cut and pull someone over, Yasmina's heart would drop. She would stare in the mirror until they were miles in the clear.

When she went back to Jamaica, Damita, Stacey, and Latoya all purchased new vehicles. But being told the reason to rent mini-vans, only Damita and Latoya understood. Stacey, she thought as long as she had a valid driver's license, it didn't matter what she drove. Now as they drove down the highway, Yasmina couldn't relax, she was anxious. When they made it to Charlotte and saw the sign that read QUEEN CITY, Yasmina sighed a slight bit. She knew they weren't in the clear, they still had another hour ahead of them. She didn't know how much longer she could tolerate Stacey.

The long journey proved successful. Pulling into Winston-Salem was a relief for Yasmina. Calling the number that Damita left her, they were given the directions to a BP Gas Station located on Martin Luther King Jr. Drive. After seeing them pull into the parking lot, Yasmina exhaled for the first time during the entire trip. The place was packed with guys riding motorcycles and phat whips. Music blared out of the speakers as men and women stood around smoking blunts and chatting. Seeing this, she knew at once this would be their next money pit.

After depositing the rest of the work at the storage unit, Yasmina checked everybody into the Adams Mark Hotel. It wasn't anything like the Fountain Bleu or the Ritz Carlton, but it was nice, and it had a jacuzzi in the room. After getting settled, they went back over to Damita's aunt's house. This is where they learned the run of things. Dalvin told them about the prices and all the dealers. He even had a couple of clients who wanted to purchase some work. From then on, he was a part of the team, and Yasmina hit him off with his first brick.

Since it was a Saturday night, Damita's cousin Tamika offered to take them out on the town. She told them about Club Alize, and they were pumped. As if having a flashback, when Yasmina walked into the club, it reminded her of when she and Selena frequented the clubs in the hood. It seemed like they were all the same. A long line of people aligned the building, and every baller had a girl or two jocking him.

Thinking that they were going to be the hottest chicks in the club, they were highly disappointed. Ballers sat at tables with three or four bottles of Dom Perignon atop, and Yasmina's face registered shock when she saw how the women dressed. They wore Roberto Cavalli, Versace dresses, Jimmy Choo Pumps, Manolo Blahnik Timbs and more. She thought that with Miami being a big city, and Winston-Salem the size of Liberty City, Carol City, and Coconut Grove all together, they wouldn't be hip to gear like that. The Prada, Dior, and Moeshe Denim they wore, were replicas or at least one of the same outfits that were worn by others inside the club.

After taking their seats, Petey Pablo's song "Helicopter" blared through the speakers. They ordered three bottles of Dom Perignon and took a few drinks, they all loosened up, and could feel the holes being burned in them by people staring. Stacey and Damita went to the dance floor, leaving Yasmina and Latoya to scope out the scenery. While everyone danced, two guys approached the table as Yasmina and Latoya talked. After chatting for a while, Hasan and Scooter exchanged numbers with them. They were two new clients to add to the list.

Around 2:30 a.m., all the action was taken outside to the parking lot. The club was closing so everyone went and stood by their rides as music played, people bragged about this and that, phone numbers were exchanged, and everyone decided where the next stop would be. But that decision didn't take long, gunshots were heard somewhere in the crowd, and everyone dispersed. The sound of sirens could be heard coming from afar. Bright and early the next morning, Yasmina prepped her girls. It was time to make money, and time to get down to business.

"Damita, how many did Dalvin say his boy want?" she asked.

"He said two, if it's some good shit."

"You know we have that bomb diggity! I assure you, he won't be disappointed," Yasmina reiterated. "I need you and Stacey to take twenty bricks from the stash and work 'em. Don't do anymore than that if you run out before I make it back. Let them wait until tomorrow," she finished saying.

She knew that business was going to boom because she'd already had half of the twenty sold. She trusted Damita to take care of everything, with the help of Dalvin. Seeing that the dealers weren't complaining about paying $21,500 dollars for the brick, she knew they'd hit the jackpot. While Stacey remained with Damita, Yasmina and Latoya took Tamika with them. They were going home shopping. One of things that Scorcher drilled into Yasmina's skull was, having a secure enough place to lay her head. With that, she wanted the place to be far enough away, but accessible to make it in an hour.

Driving around Charlotte, Yasmina felt that it would be the ideal place to find a home. It was an hour away, and it was big enough to get lost in.

Coming off the Billy Graham Expressway, she pulled into the parking lot of the Great American Convenient Store. Not knowing the city, she felt like she could get a nice layout of it by purchasing a map and an apartment guide. While driving, they checked several places, but none stood out better than the four bedroom-two bath Condo on the Westside of town. It cost $2,300 dollars a month. They dropped the first and last month's deposit, plus an extra thousand to bypass all the red tape, they set out to fill the place with accessories. After being gone for nearly eight hours before making it back to the hotel, her cell phone rang.

"Hello," she answered, seeing the unidentified number appear on her screen.

"We're on our way to the hotel, we have some good news for you," Damita said excitedly.
As she sat on the sofa, Yasmina couldn't believe her ears. As Damita explained how fast they moved the work, she just shook her head in disbelief. In Miami, it took them almost a month to move twenty-five bricks, and there, in only a couple of hours they'd managed to move twenty. What helped out big was when Dalvin introduced them to guys that bought two and three at a time. And Scooter and Hasan was in that equation.

All around town, the word was out. The chicks from Miami had the best coke. Word was, when cooking one with baking soda, you could almost bring back an extra one. And the product was still good. Dalvin had even finished the one he had, and was ready for more.

"Yas, you shoulda' seen how these cats were pulling out money," Stacey became excited.

"Did you guys run into any trouble? I mean with the guys?" Yasmina asked.

"Nope," Damita responded. "Within five hours after you left, we were finished. We really thought about going to get some more, but you said to make'em wait."

"I'm glad you waited," said Yasmina. "The idea is to keep them hungry, but not too hungry. We don't wanna move too fast, someone's bound to try us then. Plus, we don't wanna make ourselves hot."

Yasmina could tell that the Platinum Chicks didn't really understand her logic. She knew they wanted to sell as many as they could, possibly all. But it wasn't the way to have longevity in the game, and that's what she was trying to establish, she thought to herself. Making a vast quantity of money excited Damita, Latoya, and Stacey, It was more to add to their stashes. However, Yasmina always kept in mind what Scorcher told her. "Rome wasn't built in one day." Therefore, it was better to wait until the next day.

Back in Charlotte, the girls went about the task of turning their Condo into a home. Never once did Damita, Latoya, or Stacey ever imagine they'd be living in a Condo. On top of that, they all had a nice chunk safely stashed back at home. "Man, how life has changed," Damita whispered quietly to herself. With the help of Yasmina, they all felt like somebody now. They were out of the projects, and life was looking up for all of them.

The delivery truck arrived on time. The four men who unloaded the truck thought they were delivering the expensive items to a successful white occupant, but was stunned to see Yasmina and her crew waiting in the doorway. Accustomed to a posh lifestyle, Yasmina purchased a handcrafted, Italian Country Dining Table with four chairs to match, for the Dining Room. The beds for the bedrooms were made of the best hand crafted

Cherry Oak, all with a canopy covering the tops. The Den had and antique pool table that was ordered from Monarch Billiards, and a Meridian DSP-7000 Compact Digital Audio System that played movies as well as music. It sat on a Cherry Oak Stand especially designed for it. Life was good. The Platinum Chicks were balling, and it was time for money, money, and more money to be made.

"Yas, I gotta tell ya, I have the utmost respect for you," Damita raised her glass of Hennessey to her. "You didn't forget about your girls and that means more to me than you'll ever know."

There couldn't have been a better time for them to hold this conversation. "Hypnotized" by Biggie Smalls was playing in the stereo system and they all were vibing to it. Right then and there, a bond was formed that couldn't be broken.

With the place being laid out, they all piled into Stacey's Lexus and went to familiarize themselves with the Queen City. They were impressed with what they saw in Charlotte. It had a lot to offer to anyone looking for a new start, and it was only on a slightly smaller scale than Atlanta, but it was definitely happening.

After spending the day shopping, they prepared to go back to work the next day. Yasmina wanted to finish the rest of the work so everyone could go back to Miami. She wanted to see her grandmother, and knew the rest of them wanted to see their families.

Arriving at MIA International Airport, Yasmina's mind was restless. Even though it was hot and humid, she couldn't take her mind off of Stacey's comment. She really wished they had finished all the work, but things had slowed down. She hoped and prayed that they wouldn't go against her words.

Part of her reasons for going back were because of her grandmother. She wanted to make sure she was alright. The last conversation they had face to face didn't seem to sit well with her grandmother, so she wanted to check on her. However, the real reason was Damita. She could sense that Damita was missing her kids. She talked about them all the time. At times, Yasmina wished she had kids of her own, but realized that they would only slow her down. And that was the one thing she didn't need.

Many times she thought about what it would be like if her and Scorcher ever got married, but the topic was never raised. She did say that they both would have to be through with the game, if the situation ever happened. All this wishing upon a star brought a smile to her face, and her phone rang seconds later.

"I was just thinking about you," she smiled as she talked.

"Mi hope it was something' good," Scorcher replied.

"Oh it was, believe me. I can't wait until I'm back in your arms and you're holding me, making love to me," she said quietly, embarrassed by Damita's presence.

"How are tings? When will you be coming home?"

After explaining everything, she listened as he told her about the business he had to tend to in New York. He then will be heading to Chicago, and it'll be another month before they saw each other again. He really wanted to tell her that he was going to California to put some things together on Jaheim, but thought better of it. Hanging up, she felt better about her situation. This gave her more time to finish the work.

Since Yasmina and Damita were going to be gone for a week, Stacey talked Latoya into riding down to Winston-Salem with her. She had a plan, and if it worked out right, everyone would be happy.

9

"THE LICK"

"**HOLD UP**, hold up!" exclaimed Yasmina, "Stacey what the fuck are you telling me?" she screamed into the phone.

"Well, I received a call from Dalvin while you were in Miami and he said his friends wanted some work. I mean, I talked Latoya into taking me to get it from the storage unit and w….."

"Didn't I tell you to let them niggas go hungry until we made it back?" she interrupted Stacey in mid-sentence. "Why in the hell would you undermine my directions? How could you go behind my back and do that shit Stacey, huh?" Yasmina fumed.

"I'm sorry, I was just trying to….."
Yasmina was hot, she couldn't believe what she was hearing. Tired of hearing Stacey's squeaky voice, she hung the phone up in her ear. As her and Damita drove I-95 heading back to Carolina, she sat silent as she thought to herself. Damita, feeling that this wasn't the right time to ask questions, drove on without looking in Yasmina's direction. But she knew it had something to do with the drugs they left behind.

"Can you believe this bitch got robbed for four bricks?" Yasmina blurted out, breaking the silence.

"I thought you told 'em to leave it alone until we made it back."

"I did tell that bitch that, but she took it upon herself to go against my words," she retorted.   Hearing the anger, Damita continued to drive even though her nerves were beginning to bother her. She didn't know how Yasmina was going to handle the situation, but a lot of money was at stake. It was good that they were getting a price of $16,000, that enabled them to make five grand a wop. "Why would Stacey go and do something as stupid as this?" she thought to herself as her palms became sweaty. Now that this incident occurred, the trip seemed longer. Long agonizing minutes passed as silence remained in the vehicle. The only sounds to be heard were passing motorist, and the highway under the tires. Finally, after making it to Charlotte, Damita could see how anxious Yasmina was to handle the situation. Inside the condo, Stacey and Latoya were sitting in the den with the T.V. off, the audio system off, and nonchalant expressions on their faces.

"Look," Yasmina mean mugged both girls as she paced the floor holding the all black Baretta 9mm in her hand. Every now and then she would raise it as she explained things. "Y'all bitches went behind my back and took my coke, then managed to get robbed for four bricks. Now I'm out forty grand. If I didn't want to believe it, I'd say that y'all plotted and took the money, and I don't like thieves." Stacey rubbed the huge lump over her eye. "I frankly told ya'll not to fuck with it, let it sit until I made it back. Why? Why did y'all go behind my back?" she approached both girls with the gun raised.

Sobbing profusely, Stacey tried speaking but could only utter the words, "I-I-I'm sorry Yasmina. We-e just wanted to surprise you by getting rid of the rest of it. We didn't s-s-steal from you. "Sniff-sniff," she wiped her nose with a Kleenex tissue.

Yasmina continued.

"Y'all think what we're doing is cute, huh? It'll get you fame, it'll get you prestige, well I have a serious news bulletin for you. You think we can just roll into different spots in different cities and sell this shit, and everything will be hunky dory. You got the game real twisted, 'cause niggas ain't trying to hear you come and take food out of their kids' mouth. Especially a bunch of bitches, you know that's already a strike against us. They plottin' all the time, and the minute they catch yo' ass slippin', that's it, you're dead. This ain't no fucking game! I want y'all to realize two things. In this game, you'll be lucky if you make it to prison, because the other alternative is the graveyard."

"Yas, me and Stacey will pay you the money," Latoya said. "We have it in our stash back at home. We just got caught slippin'," she said matter of factly.
Seconds went by before Yasmina spoke.

"I wanna show y'all that it's not about the money. I am pissed that y'all went behind my back, though. It's the principle. You two went against my word like it didn't hold any weight. I'm the one that's helping you guys get on your feet. I think I deserve some sort of respect. If you were getting this shit from somebody else, and some shit happened, somebody wouldn't make it to see another day. I'm telling you, callousness will lead to your downfall. In this game you can't get greedy. Greed will get you all the time. Don't worry, the debt is paid. But we gotta make an example out of those niggas who did this. If not, it's hunting season and we're the prey. Y'all with me?"

Everyone agreed to be down for whatever. They didn't think that the game was that treacherous, but listening to Yasmina, the message was crystal clear. Besides, she had to know what she was talking about, they were dealing more coke than most of the guys they knew from the hood, thought Damita.

After the discussion was over and cooler heads prevailed, Latoya handed over the large black-duffle bag filled with money. Even though Yasmina was still slightly upset, she was glad to see that they'd managed to finish the work. With that, she gave each of them two-grand a piece, on top of what they'd made for themselves.

Alone in her room, Yasmina thought about the ordeal that took place. She knew the girls were hungry and trying to do good by her, but she needed them to be aware. When pointing the gun, she had no intentions of shooting them, but putting fear in them would let them see the position she held in this business. She was the boss.

Dalvin tidied up the money from the two bricks Yasmina had given him, then went for a little walk. She'd driven down to Winston-Salem with the purpose of finding information on the guys that robbed Stacey and Latoya. The trip proved worthy. It turned out that Scooter and Hasan stayed on the Southside of town. A project called Happy Hill Gardens. A buzz was circulating that they'd been doing a string of robberies and home invasions, and several incidents ended in gunplay. Hearing this, she knew they would have to bust their guns when the time came.

The stick up on Latoya and Stacey was planned. Hasan had organized it, feeling them from the first time he'd dealt with them. He saw how relaxed they went about sealing their weight, and knew it would be an easy lick. The day he called Dalvin, he and Scooter already plotted out a spot. The parking lot of "Peaches Records" was crowded, but where they'd parked their Suburban was easily accessible into the thick of traffic that led down to Peters Creek Parkway.

Stacey and Latoya sat in the Lexus, waiting patiently for the guys to show. Every second, they would look across the parking lot to see if the Black Acura was coming. Relaxed, knowing that this deal would be the last of the coke, and five extra grand in their pockets, they sat talking; unaware of the two guys creeping beside the car. Next thing they noticed, Stacey's head jerked back viciously after the huge steel barrel of the .357 magnum slammed into her skull with tremendous force. As she fought the stars that blinked in her head, she was on the verge of blacking out when she heard someone yell, "bitch, give me the bag!" Latoya, having the Desert Eagle sitting on her lap, couldn't use it. Scooter held a gun pressed to her temple. The two women sat helplessly as Scooter and Hasan made off with the coke. When they pulled into traffic, it was too late, the Suburban was long gone.

Now that Yasmina had all the information she needed, she drove back to Charlotte to formulate a plan.

Bike Rally 2001 was just kicking off, and everyone was heading to Myrtle Beach to join in on the festivities. Since Scorcher was going to be out of town and Yasmina didn't have any work, she decided that the Platinum Chicks should take a much needed break. Every year at the end of May, hundreds of thousands of black people from every state, swarmed the beach. They also came in their best; hottest bikes, cars, SUV's, and hoopties. It was a time of the year when black people came together to party and have a good time.

Since this would mark the first for the Platinum Chicks, they planned to have a ball. Everywhere they looked on the beach; someone was riding a motorcycle that was chromed from top to bottom, or driving a car that looked just as good. Luckily, Damita's cousin Tamika reserved a room for them. On the entire beach and many miles away, there wasn't any vacancy.

"Y'all see that nigga driving the Convertible Bentley," Stacey pointed. "Damn, he's fine too."

"Yeah bitch, we got eyes," said Damita. "I bet you'll give your ass to any motherfucka you thought was ballin'," she tapped her on the shoulder.

Thinking back to her days in college, Yasmina smiled to herself. She knew that a lot of females were out doing the same thing that she and Selena did years ago.

"Yo, they doin' it big down here in Myrtle Beach. This shit kind of remind me of South Beach. Look at all the black folks having a good time. This is the shit. I can imagine what the Million Man March was like." She was in awe.

Throughout the day, Yasmina and her crew enjoyed the festivities. They watched guys and girls do stunts on their bikes, and the girls were clad in only two piece-bathing suits. This impressed her, she wanted a bike now, and she imagined herself on one. Seeing a few stars ride through, pushing Maybachs, Hummers, and Bentleys, really told her what level this thing was on. So engulfed in all the action of the day, they never had a chance to make it to their room.

The next morning as the partying continued, Yasmina received a call on her cell phone. It was from Dalvin. He'd spotted Scooter and Hasan. This was good news to Yasmina's ears. The plan she formulated could now be put to use. She smiled with a devious look etched across her face.

Stepping into their designer two piece-bathing suits, the Platinum Chicks went down to join in on the action. As they made their way through the crowd, all eyes were fixated them. This happened everywhere they went. The sun was starting to beam its rays, but they were prepared. The big hats that matched their outfits almost completely hid their eyes and acted as a shield. While relaxing in the beach chairs taking in the scenery, two bikes pulled in front of them and stopped. It was Hasan and Scooter. Immediately, Stacey and Latoya noticed who they were, and whispering to Yasmina, she gave her the scoop. In their arrogance they didn't pay close attention, and went on to ask Tamika and Yasmina to ride with them. Tamika, eyeing her, wasn't sure, but followed Yasmina.

The bike ride lasted about thirty minutes. After they made it back to the strip where the rest of her crew was, she eagerly accepted Hasan's room and phone number. That's when she told Tamika her reason for accepting the ride. Not even a second later, Dalvin came over. He wanted to let them know about the guys they were riding with, but Yasmina was a step ahead of him. She produced the strip of paper with the room number and smiled.

Later that night, Yasmina and Tamika arrived at the room door of Hasan and Scooter. Knowing that things were going to get ugly, she told Tamika it was time for her to leave. Tamika, not knowing how crazy shit was going to go down, refused and said she was down for whatever. So Yasmina knocked on the door, proceeding with her intentions.

"What's up Tamika, and Yasmina?" Scooter opened the door smiling, with a lit blunt in his hand. In the background, a radio was blasting, "Danger" by Mystical.

"What's up with you?" Tamika said walking past him. Yasmina being the last one to enter.

"Your man's in the bathroom showering?" He should be out in a minute," Scooter said to Yasmina, holding a smirk on his face. "Make yourselves comfortable."

Taking a quick survey of the room, Yasmina noticed two gallons of Hennessey, a bottle of unopened Dom Perignon sitting on ice, a half pound of hydro in a clear plastic bag beside the bed, and a bunch of condoms strewn over the table. However, not one gun was in sight. Seeing everything made her mad. She knew they called themselves ballin', but it was at her expense.

Not even a second later, Hasan came strolling out the bathroom. He only wore a pair of boxers, and his skin was still wet from the shower, seeing how ripped he was, Yasmina admired his body. If she was single and wasn't there to take care of some unfinished business, she probably would've given him a taste. Not! She thought to herself. She was perfectly happy with the man she has. Passing a blunt to the women as he made them drinks, Hasan said, "Lets have some fun!" then started dancing to the music. After turning the volume as loud as it would go, he grabbed Yasmina by the hand, pulling her to him. She knew she was in the presence of the enemy, but she had to catch him off guard. So she started dancing; grinding into his midsection, causing him to become erect. Taking the act to another level, she rubbed her chest as her fingernails left scratch marks on his skin. Feeling a hand cuff her breast, her nipples started getting hard. She knew she had to play along in order for it to come across as real, so she let him fondle her nipples.

Across from her, Tamika followed cue. She rubbed Scooter all over until he was hard, making him succumb to her advances. The minute that both Scooter and Hasan's boxers were down around their ankles, the door flew open. With it being Bike Week, the entire hotel was loud, filled with rowdy people talking and playing music. Not one neighbor on any floor complained about the noise.

"Ai'ight, both of you bitch ass niggas hit the floor," Latoya gruffed as she held the Desert Eagle pointed at both guys. Stacey locked the door.

Since Hasan was the one who smacked Stacey with the gun, Latoya felt like he needed a dose of his own medicine. Treating him accordingly, she pistol whipped him while Stacey held her .380 against Scooter's head, daring him to flinch.

"What the fuck is going on?" Hasan managed to say between blows. Blood was coming from his face.

"Oh, you forgot so soon," Stacey then took her hat off exposing the black and blue mark surrounding the huge lump over her eye. "Remember me from Peaches?" she stepped over and smacked him once in the face. "You took four bricks from me. I hope you didn't think it was forgotten about."

As the assault went on, the only thing Scooter and Hasan could do was cover their heads. Not knowing things were going to get so violent, Tamika chose this time to leave. She closed the door behind her and didn't look back. While Stacey and Latoya handled business, Yasmina and Damita plugged in the irons. Forcing them to sit in the chairs, they duct taped them at the wrist and mouth. Yasmina then moved Scooter to the bed, face first. Taking the Vaseline out the bag, Yasmina scooped a hand full. Walking over to Hasan, she slowly applied it to his dick, jerking and squeezing, enough to stimulate him. Making sure he adhered to every command, Stacey held an iron close to his skin. The heat could be felt even though it wasn't touching him.

Through all the excitement, Hasan managed to grunt from anger, even though he being gagged stifled the words. The moan was uncontrollable as Yasmina continued her little ordeal. The Platinum Chicks were in a zone and bent on making a statement. Seeing Hasan responding like she wanted, she continued stroking him. His dick was standing tall now. It was time for the next step.

While Hasan moaned, Scooter squirmed trying to see what they were doing to his boy, but was shocked into stillness as the heat from the iron seared his leg. Stacey wasn't playing. As blood and puss spewed from the fresh burn, he gagged and started dry-heaving. The stench was too strong. As if the iron weren't doing enough, she smacked him beside the head a few times with the gun. He wouldn't be quiet. With everything happening, Hasan knew they wouldn't make it out alive, and his thoughts reflected back to when they robbed Latoya and Stacey.

"Aye Scooter, you know we gotta off those bitches once we lick'em for the work."

"Man, we can't do it right there in broad daylight. Too many people, plus video cameras are going to be everywhere," Scooter replied out of fear.

Before everything popped off, Scooter had a bad feeling about the lick. A few weeks prior to the lick, they'd robbed some brothas from across town for a key. Within a couple of days, Hasan was screaming broke. He knew they were pulling too many licks, and the coke problem Hasan had was beginning to get out of hand.

Shortly after that lick, someone shot up Hasan's Denali as it sat parked in front of his mother's house. Now that this was happening, he wish he'd taken the advice of his friend, and killed them when they had the chance. Through all the drama, Hasan wondered why Yasmina kept jacking his dick. But his thoughts were rudely interrupted as the steam from the hot iron caused his skin to peel and bubble. Sweat balls started forming on his head and fear came over him.

"Get your ass up, nigga!" Latoya prodded him with the gun. Without hesitation, Hasan jumped up; his hands still tied behind his back. With his dick still hard, they led him over to the bed. This is when he knew it was over. He'd robbed so many times, he felt his past had finally caught up with him. As he thought, he reflected back on when he stuck people up. He would tell his victims to face the floor and say a silent prayer. Then he'd put a slug in their heads. While he waited for everything to go blank, he was shocked when Latoya started jerking him off again. 'Why in the fuck do these bitches keep playing with me?' he thought under his breath. Seconds later he found out.

Feeling a pain like never before, Scooter's eyes bulged and he tried to let out a yell; that was cut short by tape covering his mouth. Hasan had just entered his ass. Trying desperately to break free, he turned and squirmed, but the dead weight was too much to shake. Plus Stacey held an iron to Hasan daring him to move. Latoya, in her haste to embarrass them, started pushing down on Hasan, causing him to go deeper and deeper into Scooter. They all were getting a laugh from this. A while later, Latoya noticed Hasan jerking, so she removed her hands. Seeing his body hump involuntarily, she knew he was releasing himself into Scooter. As it happened, Yasmina started snapping Polaroid shots of them.

Knowing that shattering their egos would be enough, Yasmina placed the photos inside her bag. She felt like they were paid back for what happened, and told the girls to clean the place up. Revenge on these two felt good. It was her first and real aggressive act, and the power behind it was thrilling. She now understood the affect money had over people. However, Hasan had a different outlook. He wondered why they just didn't kill them. It would've been better than humiliating them like that. If they lived, everything he'd do from this day forward would be to bring pain to them. Even if it took killing their families, where ever they may be.

Thinking the pictures were going to be message enough, she planned on having them shown to everyone around town, but she wasn't thinking clearly.

"Look, we can bounce. We have enough to ruin these muthafuckas," she said.

"Hold up!" chimed Latoya. "We can't let them live. Have you forgotten this is some serious shit we're dealing with? It's the game and we gotta finish what we'd started. If we don't, it'll come back to haunt us. "With that, she grabbed Damita's .380 and popped off two shots into the pillow. One for Scooter, and one for Hasan.

Seeing this, Yasmina became speechless. As feathers slowly drifted over the place, she stood wide mouthed, in awe. The blood and brain matter spattered everywhere. After taking the duct tape off, they made sure to clean the room spotless. They didn't need to leave anything that could be used as evidence. Walking out the door, Yasmina placed a do not disturb sign on it, and the Platinum Chicks left. They were made women now.

Ten

"THE PROPOSAL"

Scorcher hugged Yasmina's naked body as his fingers gently stroked each fiber of her hair. They'd just finished having sex, and now they lay embraced in the moment. Being apart for so long made them realize how much they really cared for each other. But there was still work to be done, so they went about the task at hand.

The trip to Ocho Rios was a topic discussed, and the vacation was going to be one very much needed. While chatting, Yasmina told Scorcher about the situation they ran across, and by the look on his face, he wasn't feeling what she was saying. Attempts to convince him that they handled business didn't come across to him like it was handled in a professional manner.

"Why didn't you just kill them and get it over with?" he asked.

"I wanted to show them that we weren't to be taking lightly just because we're females," she responded sounding confused, thinking that he would've been happy to know that she got revenge. She couldn't understand why he was getting upset.

"Shaw'ty, there's one ting' you need to know," he paused, letting his words sink in, then spoke. "When you do dirt, you get dirt. Mi am glad that you handled your business, but you went about it unprofessionally. There were too many risks. Hotel Security, the guys could've had other friends coming through, not to mention, you risked leaving something lying around.

And it could have your prints all over it. If you have to do tings' like that, do it on your playing field, that way time is on your side, you clean the place without rushing, and no one can point a finger saying they saw you in the vicinity. That's all mi saying." He tilted her chin with the flick of his finger.

Hearing what was said, she knew he was right. They were very careless, and lucky that someone didn't hear them. Next time, she thought to herself, they would just handle business and bounce. If there ever came a next time.

At 10:30 a.m. Air Jamaica descended onto the runway, skidding to a halt in front of the terminal. All thoughts of the previous conversation disappeared and her tension subsided. It was time to focus on having a good time. As the taxi drove them through the winding hills, she couldn't help but admire the beautiful scenery. The farther they went up in elevation, the smaller everything beneath them looked, and to see the vast blue ocean below, blew her mind. It was picturesque.

As they walked along the beaches that were covered by black sand, cascades of waves crashed at their feet, splashing water on them. Far enough from everyone but in their own privacy, Yasmina and Scorcher stood face to face, engulfed in a conversation. The reggae band could clearly be heard in the background, as well as the people who were out enjoying themselves. A small single engine airplane kept hovering over in the air, going un-noticed with a banner attached that trailed in the wind. As Scorcher caressed her hands, the DJ made an announcement. Seeing him point towards the sky, everyone looked up in that direction. This also caused Yasmina to look. And when she did, she couldn't get a word out.

"Huhgh!" was the only sound that came out of her as she stood with her mouth wide open. The banner read, "YASMINA, WILL YOU MARRY ME?"

Turning back to Scorcher, she found him on his knees holding a five carat ring in hand.

"Oooh baby," she cried as she jumped on him giving him a hug. "Yes, yes I would be glad to carry your last name." She then kissed him.

Hugging and dancing in each other's arms, they celebrated in happiness. After making it back to their hotel room, an intense session of sex consummated the engagement. The big date was set for January 1, 2002. Knowing that marriage was something sacred, they vowed to be finished with the drug game before tying the knot. Marital bliss would be spent without any parts of that life in it, so they could enjoy life together, forever

For either of them, there couldn't be any wasting of time. There were many loose ends that needed tying up. Scorcher still had a huge shipment that he and Yasmina needed to finish, Jaheim hadn't been found, and Shotty Dread still hadn't been told of what was going to happen in the near future. Yasmina, being the good hearted person she is, wasn't about to abandon her crew. Figuring it would take at least eight more months to finish everything, she planned three more big runs. This would help them secure enough money to live a nice and comfortable life for themselves. It was her way of showing her appreciation, and helping them get on their feet.

Yasmina was taken aback when Scorcher popped the question. A month prior, the thoughts of them settling down and having kids ran through her mind, but it wasn't something that she entertained seriously. She figured they both weren't ready for such a step, but knowing what she knows now, time was of the essence.

****

For months, Scorcher had been trying to find a way to tell Shotty Dread that he wanted out of the business. He knew it would be a difficult task because nothing was simple when it came to Shotty Dread.

"Boo, what's wrong?" Yasmina asked seeing him in deep thought.

"Mi just tinking. Mi trying to find a way to tell him that mi want out, mi want out the game forever." He sat with a look of confusion on his face.

"Can't you just quit?" asked Yasmina.

Scorcher knew he couldn't make her understand, this was another part of the game she was green to. Luckily it was him that she was getting her work from, because she wouldn't stand a chance if it were someone else, he thought, as he looked through her.

"Shaw'ty, it's not easy as you tink'. A man like Shotty Dread, there's no quitting. Besides, I'm indebted to him forever."

This, she really didn't understand. As far as she knew, Scorcher paid him every time he was finished with a shipment, and he never mentioned anything about owing him a dime. She listened as he told her about the $37 million he had in different offshore accounts, and wondered why he could still possibly be indebted for the rest of his life.

For the past six months, Scorcher had been buying his coke from a Colombian dealer named Poncho. Getting it at wholesale price was far better than what Shotty Dread was charging, even though the price was lovely.   This opportunity came when he made the decision to quit the game. Only thing he was doing now, was stacking his paper, and securing his future with Yasmina.

He went on to tell her about how Poncho would smuggle the drugs on the island using Lobster Boats that held bails of uncut cocaine. He knew all this information was over her head, but also knew that divulging the information to her showed that there was nothing to hide. Listening intently to her man discussing the business in detail, Yasmina clearly could sense the danger now; it was on a level she never anticipated.

After talking for a while, she still wasn't satisfied with some aspects of what Scorcher had told her, he explained everything about how dangerous the game was and how the drug made it from point A to point B, but not why he owed Shotty Dread his life. With all the money he had, she knew he could leave Jamaica forever and never be found again, hut he knew different.

Finally, opening up and laying all of his cards on the table, he told her the reason.

"Shaw'ty," Scorcher reached a hand out to keep Yasmina from running out the door, but it was too late, "wh—what's wrong?"

He found her sitting under a coconut tree, crying her eyes out. The minute he knelt to ask her what was wrong, she lashed out at him.

"How could you?" She smacked him across his face. "I can't believe it was you, how can you live with yourself?" She cried harder as she placed her face in her hands.

Scorcher didn't know what to make of the situation. All he knew was, the minute he told Yasmina the real reason behind owing Shotty Dread for the rest of his life, she ran out the room. He was truly confused as he stood watching her cry. He wasn't alone. Her situation was just as grave as his, but on a deeper level. As she sat crying under the tree, she tried sorting out her feelings. Here she was, madly in love with the man who was partly responsible for her parents' death. This made her shake like a frightened puppy. Her emotions peaked and every time Scorcher touched her, she jumped, out of hate, anger, and an admixture of fear.

Seeing how distraught she was, and not knowing the reason, he knelt down and asked her what the problem was as he gently cupped her chin so their eyes would meet. The response was enormous. What he heard was a vicious blow to his ears. It couldn't be, he thought as he staggered away disconcerted. 'How could it had been her parents, why?' he asked himself.

Yasmina in her sadness, relayed the story of her parents' death to Scorcher. Seeing the shocked expression on his face, told her everything he needed to know. He was the one that murdered them as they sat waiting at a stoplight in Trenchtown. Call it coincidence, because he remembered it like it happened the day before.

Knowing this was a delicate and fragile situation, he had to handle Yasmina carefully. For one, he now feared losing her because of something in the past, and two, she knew too much about him, his life of drugs, money, and murder. Leading her back into the room after pleading and begging, he sat her on the bed and tried to make her understand why he did the murderous deed.

"Shaw'ty, mi know mi cannot correct what mi did, but mi need you to listen, let me explain," he held her attention before going on.

Explaining about being poor and watching his father get killed for being ten dollars short on drug money owed to a dealer, he succeeded in getting her attention. This ordeal left him and his mother to fend for themselves, and he was just a kid at the time. He could still remember nights when his mother prostituted to put food on the table. However, the trauma of it came when she performed the acts right before his eyes.   This happened daily under the roof of the cramped one bedroom shanty. One night as a customer became aggressive, his mother struggle to fight for her life. Scorcher, merely a teenager, hid under the bed and watched in horror. The guy kept complaining that he didn't get to have an orgasm and swore that he would kill her if she didn't let him.

At the time, Scorcher was too young to understand what the sexual terminology meant, but he knew well enough that his mother was being violated and there was nothing he could do about it. Seeing them scuffle; glass falling and breaking upon contact on the wooden floor, he crawled as far back into the dark corner under the bed as he could. His mother told him to do this long before any of the clients showed up. After about five minutes, this smell of blood invaded the tiny, cluttered, and hot room. A deadly silence followed. Watching two huge feet make it closer and closer to the bed, Scorcher trembled as fear gripped him. He couldn't hear his mother nor see her, and this frightened him. When the man knelt on one knee, Scorcher took this opportunity to run. Sprinting from under the bed, he ran for the door; only to be drugged to the floor by his shirt collar. That's when he made the gruesome discovery, his mother's dead body was lying on a table with her throat slashed from ear to ear.

Just as the sharp and bloody blade was about to come down across his, the wooden door flew off the hinges, leaving splinters all across the floor. Two shots rang out and the guy fell to the floor-dying in his own blood. From that day on, Scorcher was indebted to Shotty Dread.

To earn a living, he started working as a runner a week after the burial. To graduate and make it to the ranks of a dealer, Scorcher had to first, prove his loyalty to hhim. Independence Day was soon to be celebrated again, and Shotty Dread would use this momentous occasion for the initiation of Scorcher. That night, armed with AK-47's, they waited for their victims. The taxi had just pulled up at the stop light with three occupants inside. Unaware of anything bad about to happen, they sat talking. This is when Shotty Dread and Scorcher appeared. Giving the order, they pressed the triggers of the automatic machine guns. The slaughter lasted only minutes as they dumped over a hundred bullets into taxi, killing everyone inside. That night, three innocent people lost their lives, and Scorcher was promoted to dealer. It's very strange how fate would bring two people together, he thought as he witnessed tears after tears fall from Yasmina's eyes.

Even though he'd given an explanation, it wasn't enough to make her feel any different than she felt at the moment. Her anger over her parents' death resurfaced, and she resented Scorcher for taking them away.

Being in the same room but both in different states of minds, a separation needed to happen. Scorcher kept wondering why of all people, it had to be Yasmina's parents. Yasmina on the other hand, had the same thoughts but was indecisive about the course of action to be taken. Confused and needing space, she decided to take a long walk on the beach. As she slowly strolled the shore looking out beyond the vastness of water, tears fell to the ground. The tears were partly shed because of the discovery, but they were also shed because of what she was planning to do. In this matter, apologies couldn't be accepted, she thought as she watched a seagull scoop a fish out the water. There was only one way to ease the pain.

"Yasmina, what's wrong? Why are you crying? Did that nigga put his hands on you?" Selena kept questioning. She was frantic hearing her best friend crying.

Having so much pressure on her, she needed to talk to someone before she made her decision. She couldn't call her grandmother and tell her about what she discovered, so she dialed up Selena. She knew Selena would help rationalize the situation.

"No," she stuttered as the word struggled to come out. After explaining everything, even her thoughts of what to do, she sat and listened to Selena.

"Yas, I know you love him and he just proposed to you and all, but if you wanna come back home, my door is always open for you. I know how you feel and don't blame you for wanting to kill him, but think about it; you'll be lowering yourself to his level. I don't think you parents would want that. So far whatever it's worth, just take time to think about what you're going to do. Another thing, I can't tell you what to do in your relationship, but I'll be a friend that offers advice. I'm saying this because I don't want you to make a decision, and later blame me for taking you away from your happiness. Fate has away of bringing people together, and taking them apart. For now, don't make any irrational decisions. Think things over and then come to a conclusion."

"I know whatchu' mean, thanks girl. This shit just blows my mind and I needed someone to talk to. Lord knows I couldn't call grandma, her ass would've been on a plane with gun in hand." They both laughed. After talking, she felt better

11

"TROUBLE'S BREWING"

"Yas, you heard what happened to Stacey?" Damita ran in the living room, as she talked on the phone.

"Nah, what happened?"

"She got busted in Opalocka with four bricks. The FEDS have her under a two million dollar bond," exclaimed Damita.

"How in the hell was she busted? She didn't have any work with her when she went back to visit her family, did she?" Yasmina asked confused.

Not feeling like her usual self, Yasmina laid back. For the past week, she'd been feeling sick for no particular reason. Ever since she left Ocho Rios, her stomach had been feeling queasy, and she'd vomited twice. Little did she know, she'd let her guard down and Stacey took advantage of the opportunity.

When Yasmina came back to Charlotte and informed them that she had two hundred bricks in storage, a light shined in Stacey's mind. She knew how careless Yasmina was when it came to keeping an account of the work. As long as the money was right, she was happy. Feeling like it was a time to make a come up, she made a quick stop by the storage unit and collected fifty bricks for herself. All the girls knew the combination to the master lock.

Feeling like they were the ones doing the majority of the work, Stacey figured she deserved to

103

enjoy the fruits of their labor as well as Yasmina. She was going to do her own thing.

Still a bit under the weather, Yasmina didn't have a clue at first, about being short fifty bricks. She'd taken a few extra days to lie around, in hopes that her sickness would go away. Thinking to herself, she noticed how meticulous Stacey had become after hearing that there was only going to be three more runs. A lot of animosity came from her, but Yasmina overlooked it. Damita and Latoya were a different story all together. They congratulated Yasmina on her engagement and thanked her for helping them get on their feet.

"Where's Latoya, anyway?" Yasmina asked, since they were talking about Stacey.

"She's on her way down here now. Her flight should be arriving at the airport in two hours," said Damita.

Since Yasmina was just making it back from her vacation in Jamaica, Stacey and Latoya felt they should take a short one before things got cranked up again. While back in Miami, Stacey called Latoya asking her to make a run with her, and to bring some heat. Hearing this puzzled Latoya. She wondered why Stacey would want her to bring a gun, did she have some work with her? Did she have beef with someone in the old neighborhood or what? She thought to herself as she sat with her mother.

Before taking the trip back to Miami, Latoya was approached by Stacey. She informed Latoya of what was about to go down, and asked if she wanted in. Latoya, not really knowing if she was serious, brushed the comment off and told Stacey that she had a flight out and wouldn't miss it. She didn't feel like taking the sixteen-hour car ride. As she drove across town to Stacey's new apartment, her mother informed her that Stacey was locked up in jail. The FEDS busted her making a sale to two undercovers. Hearing this, she immediately called Damita.

Thinking about the severity of the situation, Yasmina was shaken a little. For one, she didn't know Stacey's character. She wondered if she would talk. She also knew that if anyone went close to the jail in attempts to bond her out, the FEDS would nab them too. Then something occurred to her.

"Damita, take me to the storage unit."

Even though she was sick, she had to follow her instincts. A gut feeling told her that something wasn't right. After they made it to the storage located on Tyvola Road, Yasmina couldn't believe what she was seeing.

"Fuck!" she cursed, "can you believe this, that bitch hit me up for fifty bricks. I knew something wasn't right when you said she had work with her." She looked at Damita, "When I mentioned that we only had three more runs, I could tell she wasn't feeling what I was saying. She was too pressed about what she was going to do. Shit!" Yasmina pounded her fist into the aluminum wall.

Since the situation was already heated, Damita didn't add anything. She knew Yasmina was ready to literally kill someone. Knowing Latoya's plane would touch down, soon, they drove to the airport. Taking some precautionary measures, they made plans to move the work to a different locale. And in the event, Yasmina said, "fuck Stacey and her bond," to no one in particular. She knew the FEDS knew everything about them now.

Despite everything that happened within the last few weeks, the Platinum Chicks did what they were good at, they hustled. Since they were now one person shy, this was opportunity for Dalvin to come up. Yasmina started giving him five bricks.

Hanging out in the Queen City was on a different scale than in Winston-Salem. In Charlotte, the Platinum Chicks balled where the real ballers did their thing and basketball players alike, not to mention WNBA Stars. This particular night, they decided to hangout, and the club was off the hook when they walked in. Everywhere they turned, girl groupies as well as guy groupies aligned the halls, waiting to see if they could be noticed.

This wasn't the case for the PLATINUM CHICKS. They were the ones who decided how things would end at the end of the night. After taking their seats, Yasmina ordered two bottles of Dom Perignon. Again, they were dressed to impress, and weren't about to let the troubles of Stacey ruin their night. As the party went on, everyone was dancing and having fun, but Yasmina couldn't seem to get comfortable. For some reason, an eeriness kept making her feel like she was about to vomit. Seconds later, she was headed toward the bathroom.

"Girl, you okay?" asked Latoya, seeing her friend dry heave into the toilet. The other girls in the bathroom looked on, being nosey.

"Yeah, I'm ai'ight," Yasmina turned the faucet on to wash her hands.

Having been through this same episode twice, Damita knew exactly what was going on. Yasmina was pregnant. It didn't dawn on her before, but as she looked at her slightly swollen face and hands, it was too apparent. They made it back to the table. They were shocked to find two females occupying their seats. Damita, feeling like they were being disrespected, was about to protest when Yasmina told them it was alright. She wasn't in the mood to fight and there was extra space anyway.

After offering them drinks, she made them feel comfortable. This was merely a plot to find new connections, but what she heard threw her off. Off the rip, the girls started talking about all the superstar ballers that were in the club. Yasmina knew they were straight up groupies then. The ultimate came when one of the females inquired about which star bought the two bottles of Dom Perignon. This caused a gaze to emit from Yasmina, to Latoya , then to Damita. As if rehearsed, they each burst out laughing. Little did the females know, they were sitting with a bunch of superstars themselves, Ghetto Superstars.

The night came to an end, and everyone needed to eat their highs down. IHOP on Independence was the place of choice. For Yasmina, this was a relief. Still not facing the fact of pregnancy, she figured a little food would do the trick. Besides, the only thing wrong with her was a flu bug. At least, she wanted to think that.

"Yas," said Damita, "I don't know who you think you're fooling, but you're pregnant." She eyed her suspiciously.

"No I'm not, it's just a bug that I caught when I got back from Jamaica, and that weed we smoked tonight didn't help either."

"Umm-huh, tell me anything. Don't forget, I have two boys, so I know." Back at the condo, Yasmina lay on the bed thinking. I can't be pregnant. I hadn't had my period in a month, but that's normal. Some women don't get them for months at a time. Besides, the timing isn't right. There's only seven more months and we'll be finished." She went to sleep that night in a funk.

Awaking the next morning, she had a terrible hangover. The drinks she had at the club really did something terrible to her head. She went in the bathroom, but the apartment seemed too quiet to her. She knew Damita and Latoya were normally stirring by this time, but the place was quiet. After checking Damita's room and seeing that she was still knocked out, she closed the door and went to see if Latoya was up, but she saw something strange.

Trying her best to stifle her laugh, she barged into Damita's room, snatching her out of bed. When she opened Latoya's door, the two of them burst out laughing, almost on the brink of tears. Latoya was ass naked, slobbering out the mouth, lay with her arms wrapped around the body of one of the females that sat at their table in CJ's. The loud snoring made Yasmina wonder how the girls could sleep amidst all that noise. Thinking back to the episode that happened back in Miami, she could remember the incident at Club Rolex all too well. She finally figured it out. Latoya was into women.

Damita started telling her about Latoya's stint in Juvenile hall. It happened after she got into an altercation, and ended up slicing a girl with a razor. She was sentenced to three years. While serving time, she was turned out by one of the older females, and since then, held an interest in women. This freaked Yasmina out.

Stacey sat in the small cramped 7x 9 cell, mad at herself. Claustrophobia had long begun to set in, and it was not a good feeling. The past couple of days had been hell for her. The only thing she could do was reflect back on how Yasmina helped bring her out of the trenches, and how greed now overwhelmed her into biting the hand that fed her. After safely making it back to Miami, loaded with the stolen bricks, she'd run into a little trouble at the home front.

While walking into the once new nice two-bedroom apartment that was only shared with her mother, Stacey's eyes focused on something that reminded her of scenes in New Jack City. The living room resembled an alley; trash and clothes strewn all over, the house reaped of old-spoiled food. However, what surprised her most was seeing her mother and her junkie boyfriend in a comatose state, as two needles dangled from their veinless arms. This confirmed her first thoughts. They found her stash.

Although she thought she had it safely hidden, an afterthought told her to check it, just in case they hadn't found it. Climbing the foldout ladder that was used as an entrance into the attic, the first thing she noticed was an array of boxes that were out of place. Panic started to set in. The last time she was there, which was almost to two months ago, everything was neat and in it's place. Seeing this, she knew something wasn't right, since being reunited with Yasmina, she'd been able to send her mother $500 dollars every week. Some of it was to take care of bills, and the rest was for personal necessities such as hygiene product, food and maybe a movie.

"Dam!", she cursed aloud, seeing that the once almost full duffle bag was a little on the light side, the $75,000 had diminished into a mere$32,000 and change. She felt like going down stairs and ending it for her mother and boyfriend. But she couldn't, she loved her mother too much. For the past year, her mother had been trying to change her life. Being a coke and crack addict for the last ten years was a hard road to conquer, that's why Stacey was proud when her mother willingly enrolled into the Drug Rehabilitation Program, and the fact that she'd left her boyfriend. Coming back home and finding her stash as low as it was, hurt her.

Frustrated, she decided to make a run. One quick drop would net the loss. And she knew where she could easily make the money. Knowing she would need some back up, she called Latoya. Latoya was the one who told her about the guys who lived in the apartment complex that had one way to enter and leave. Not being able to get up with Latoya in time, she made the move by herself. Desperation was setting in. As fate would have it, when she made the sale to the two guys, they flashed badges that read F.B.I...

As she sat in the small cell, she wished she never crossed Yasmina. To make matters worse, she kept getting visits from the same two agents that arrested her, and the words they kept saying played over and over in her head. "The first person on the bus gets the ride." This made her think that they had more information that they were letting on. "What are they trying to tell me?" She racked her brains as she sat on the hard bunk. They kept pestering her to divulge any information that could possibly help her out, but they didn't name anyone in particular. This scared her. She didn't know how the government agents worked when trying to gather information, but the way President Bush handled situations in Iraq, she had a hunch. Coming to a conclusion, she decided to wait. She would see exactly how much they knew, she then lay back on the flat pillow.

The next day, the jingling of keys could be heard outside her door.

"Ms. Adams, come with me." The guard didn't smile as she placed handcuffs on her wrists, then ushered her down the long hallway,

"Take a seat!" It wasn't an offer from the agent as he glared at her, it was a command.

"I'm Agent Wallace and this is Agent Vincent," he pointed to his partner. "We talked with you the other day, we didn't seem to get it far with you, but I hope you understand the seriousness of your situation. Ms. Adams, I'm not going to beat around the bush with you. I'm gonna be blunt. You're in a lot of trouble. If you're upfront with us and tell us what we want to know, I promise you, we'll help you out," the tall black and lanky agent said.

"What do you mean you can help me out?" Stacey wanted to be clear on things.

"As you already know, we're Federal Agents, this is a Federal Case, and we can make thing happen. Good or bad." Agent Vincent spoke for the first time, "As of this very moment, you're facing twenty years to life in prison for the drugs we have on you," he lied. "If there's anything more we find later, then they'll be added to your charges. I also would like to inform you that you can have a lawyer present. But if I were you, I'd hear me out. Cooperate and give us what we want, and we'll guarantee leniency. First person on the bus gets the ride!"

Here we go with that shit again, thought Stacey. She started perspiring and sweat dripped form her armpits. The two men who wore blue jeans and plain white T-shirts with badges around their necks, made her nervous. There was no telling what they would do.

Being bound, gagged and tortured by electricity was the first thing to run through her mind. There was no telling how far they'd go.

"Do you know who these young ladies are, Ms. Adams?" Agent Vincent slapped the pictures atop the table, bringing Stacey back to reality. Seeing this made things clearer now. She knew why they kept saying, "First person on the bus gets the ride." They were on to the PLATINUM CHICKS.

"No I don't, am I suppose to know them?" she kept an expressionless face.

"Are you sure?" The agent held the picture right before her eyes. "Think, take a closer look, something might come to you," he tried using psychology.

"I want you to be very sure, remember, annnny(stressing the word **any**) information you give us will help you out," he smiled.

For a second, Stacey pondered whether she should tell them what they wanted to know. However, at the last minute, she decided to consult a lawyer.

"That's your decision as well as your choice, but there's one more photo I want you to take a look at."

When Stacey saw the photo of her and the PLATINUM CHICKS standing outside the storage unit, she almost shit on herself. The picture was taken around the time they'd rented the Condo. Her baby blue Lexus was parked in front.

"I want a lawyer," she demanded loudly.

"Have it your way, but I wouldn't take this charge alone if I were you. You're gonna do a lot of time behind bars protecting your friends. Save yourself! Oh and one more thing, the offer still stands. First person on the bus gets the ride." Both agents chuckled as they walked out the door.

Left sitting alone in the small interrogation room, she felt abandoned. Her spirit was crushed. She knew the Feds had her red-handed, and her future lay in the palms of their hands. There was a decision to make. She could either do life in prison, or tell on her friends. Either way, someone would get hurt.

****

Before passing up all the drama and making it to the end of the block, Damita glanced into the rearview mirror only to see Dalvin staring at them. Their eyes locked on each other.

"That bitch snitched us out!" Damita exclaimed to Latoya in anger.

"Why do you think that?"

"Quit being naïve, Latoya. Why the fuck did they just lock my cousin up? The Feds! I hope Yasmina's alright. Stacy's been down there a month and we hadn't done as much as send her a dime. I can imagine why she told."

"We don't really know if she told or not," Latoya stated. "But we can't risk going down there ourselves. Besides, when she took the work, she wasn't coming back, she was getting ready to do her own thing. If I was Yasmina, I wouldn't send her ass a penny. Plus, the Feds are waiting on anybody to show up claiming they know her. And that's your ass!" She drove, not uttering another word.

"We gotta convince Yasmina to let that Condo go. It's hot now. Stacey's probably told them everything," added Damita.

113

"Yeah, we need to bounce to another state or something," Latoya chimed in.

Frightened, Damita called her apartment in Miami. She needed to make sure her mother and kids were safe. After confirming it, they drove the rest of the trip to Charlotte in silence.

12

"VIBES"

"Shaw'ty, are you alright?   You look beat," Scorcher said, noticing the worn look on Yasmina's face.

"I'm just tired.   A lot of shit happened on this run," he laid across he bed in exhaustion.

"You wan' talk 'bout it?" He sensed a little aggression in her voice, and decided to approach the subject delicately.

"Not right now baby, I need to rest. We'll talk later, okay?" she rubbed her fingers through his dreads.

Wanting to escape everything, she filled the Jacuzzi bathtub with Strawberry Bath and Body wash. Sitting in the hot water did wonders for her.   The vibrations from the jet motors made her relax, and for a moment she drifted to sleep.   Cleaning herself off, she walked back into the bedroom, only to be accosted by Scorcher.   He slid his arms around her bare tummy.

"Shaw'ty, you're putting on weight.   Are you pregnant?" he jokingly asked.   Not knowing how to answer and being caught off guard, Yasmina replied, "No, I'm just bloated, that's all."   Thought she didn't want to tell him just yet, she felt bad for keeping it a secret.

That night after sex, Scorcher held a puzzled look upon his face.   All during intercourse, Yasmina acted as if he was killing her.   She wasn't able to take all of him, and she moaned until tears fell.   Then, the sex felt different altogether.   It was better more… he couldn't quite put a finger on it as he sat thinking back to the moment.

Knowing that he was bothered by their sex, she decided to broach a topic that would veer his thoughts. She talked about the wedding, and where it would be held. She also told him she wanted her grandmother to spend a couple months with them. She knew her grandmother would be able to help her through the pregnancy.

Since it was time to bear good news, he mentioned that he would be tying up loose ends with Shotty Dread. He'd already contacted a realtor and purchased a $1.5 million dollar home in Miami's Coconut Groves. Hearing this brought a smile to her face. They would be free of Shotty Dread forever, and could live life as a normal couple. Reaching for the straps on his Sean John, silk robe, she removed the soft material and placed her warm lips around his penis. She knew they both had problems, but minute by minute, they seemed to get better. Hiding his fears, Scorcher knew the task wasn't going to be an easy one.

****

The three weeks she'd been back in Jamaica flew by. With all the talk of marriage and the preparations for moving to Miami, she almost forgot about her flight. It was leaving from Norman Manley Airport Sunday night.

The cars and all the furniture was already in route by boat, and would be waiting for Yasmina when she arrived at the docks. When Scorcher told her about Shotty Dread's temper, she thought back to Poncho, the Colombian

Although Poncho was of Colombian decent, he lived in Jamaica all of his life. By

happenstance, he began working for Shotty Dread. As time went on, he was beginning to

feel like he wasn't getting his money's worth, and started dealing with the Colombians

himself. Over time, he netted millions of dollars. This led into loss of money for Shotty

Dread.   And it was then he'd received the tips of Poncho's treachery.

One weekend, Shotty Dread threw a party aboard his 205-foot Yacht, invited a few Jamaican associates, Colombian, guest-men and women, and his trusting Lieutenants. The boat was headed for Montego Bay an hour before the sun began to set. The rays bounced off the rippling waters, leaving a beautiful imprint in the memories of the guest on board. Everyone was enjoying the spectacular sight. As the redness overshadowed the crisp dark waters, the vessel sailed farther out into the vast ocean. Once they were far enough from anyone and everything, Shotty informed the passengers of the show he was about to present.

As two of his trusting Lieutenants returned, murmurs of shock escaped the crowd. A blindfolded man was being led at gunpoint. His hands bound and body beaten, everyone could tell the display wasn't going to be what they expected. Barely conscious, Poncho managed to plea for his life. Aghast, the murmurs from the spectators turned into silent whispers of sorrow.

When Shotty Dread raised his machete, the only thing that could be heard was the whistling of birds flying overhead, and the vessel, barely audible as they hummed across the water.

"What stands before you today ladies and gentlemen, is what mi call a traitor." He looked to each and every person. "Mi give this mon' a life when he had not a ting'. A vagrant on the streets of Kingston, when mi invited him into the organization. Mi made him who he is today, a rich man. He has a business, a family, and money, thanks to me. Mi give him the world, and now mi must take it back. Dis' traitor started doing business behind my back with my friend Flacco," he pointed to Flacco who stood beside the rail. He swallowed hard, knowing his life could be in danger as well. "Come here Flacco," Shotty Dread ordered.

While the two conversed, the boat came to a slow-creeping stop. The sun, now falling further into the water, left an eerie presence over each passenger. Out of nowhere, a big splash was heard. Everyone raced to the side to see what hit the water so viciously. It was bloody meat being dumped into the murky abyss. Seconds later, they were astonished to see sharks appear in a frenzy, after smelling the blood.

Everyone waited in anticipation as Shotty Dread walked around the deck. He leaned on his hand crafted cane, and continuously smacked the machete against his leg. Starting his speech once again, he informed everyone what he was about to do would happen to anyone who betrayed him. With one deft swing, Poncho's right foot was severed completely off. A shrieking yelp followed as he cried out in pain. Blood sprayed the deck, as well as the passengers.

118

Walking over to Flacco, he wiped the blood stained blade on the lapel of his jacket. With the motion of a finger, one of his Lieutenants hoisted Poncho onto a hook, and pressed the button on a lever. When the whirring of the motor ceased, the only sounds to be heard were coming from Poncho, who now was dangling inches from the shark-infested water. Resembling a bunch of tadpoles in a small stream, the sharks were in a frenzy. Poncho's fresh blood had them irate as they flailed through the water attempting to taste the source of the fresh drips of blood.

Disoriented and in distress, he could hear the water in its violent undertow, and knew his life would soon be cut short. This brought on fear. He couldn't control himself, and soiled his pants with urine and feces. The lever slowly lowered, causing his body to become partly submerged. He felt the coldness instantly. A second later, a million teeth attacked his legs while his upper torso was still above water and twisted like a rag doll as the sharks ripped at him. He yelled and cried out to unheard ears, and moments later, numbness came over him. Shredded and mangled, his half-corpse remained above water as sharks took turns ripping his intestines out. They literally jumped out the water to eat the meal that hung by a hook.

The onlookers watched in horror as the sharks and the ocean swallowed up Poncho. As the blood-daring feat came to an end, Shotty Dread informed them that this was going to be the form of payment for anyone who crossed him, even the Colombians.

Hearing how vicious and callous Shotty Dread was, Yasmina became very frightened for Scorcher's life. Understanding fully how dangerous he was, she did everything; plead, begged, and cried, in hopes that he would change his mind about meeting him. She just wanted him to board the plane with her and forget he ever existed. However, Scorcher new different. When dealing with power and money, certain lines are not to be crossed.

If they are breached, you will be running for the rest of your life. Therefore, he had to deal with Shotty Dread once and for all. If he took him lightly, he'd end up paying with his life.

Yasmina never had any dealings with Shotty Dread, but she had a brief encounter with him before. It was on a Saturday morning as she swam alone in the Olympic size pool. Clad in only a two piece bathing suit, she waited and waited for Scorcher to come join her. Becoming restless and tired of waiting, she was about to step out, when she noticed a pair of eyes undressing her. Standing with an Onyx Handmade Cane was Shotty Dread. His dreads were naughty and lapped to the center of his back, one leg visually shorter than the other, and a menacing scowl was etched permanently across his face. This left an imprint embedded in her mind forever.

"Baby, don't meet with him. It's my last day and I want to spend it with you. Besides, my plane leaves in a couple hours. If you make reservations now, you could still leave with me. Just do it, something's fishy about him wanting to meet with you all of a sudden," her eyes pleaded with him.

"Baby, no worry, mi got dis ting' under control. By Monday, Kingston will be a ting' of the past, we move on to bigger and better tings,'" said Scorcher.

Checking her watch, it was something she'd been doing for the past couple of hours. Six o'clock was fast approaching, and Scorcher hadn't returned from his meeting with Shotty Dread. This worried her. Calling his cell phone, she got no answer. As fear set in, she rubbed her barely protruding belly. She wished she'd told him about her pregnancy. Maybe, just maybe, it would've changed his mind, she thought as tears fell on her shirt.

13

"Desperate Deception"

"Why ya wan'do dat, mon?" Shotty Dread started menacingly into Scorcher's eyes, "me give ya everyting you ever wanted."

"No disrespect to you brethren, but mi wan' to settle down and raise a family. Away from Jamaica. Mi don't wan' to sell drugs for the rest of mi life, mi wan' to be legit," he nervously replied.

"Bloodclot, you forget who made you, mon?" He spat venomously. "It was me. You were just a ragamuffin when I pulled you out the gutter. Mi got you dat nice home you live in, the nice cars, and even the money. In case you forget already, mi was the one who saved your life when dat wretched mon killed your prostitute mother."

The last thing said was a powerful and hurtful blow. Scorcher knew the topic was going to come up. It was a lifeline Shotty Dread used every time he needed some leverage. Knowing he would basically be provoked by being belittled and ridiculed was the reason he chose the Café Shop on Wildman Street as a prime location to meet. It was located in a highly concentrated business area, and a police station sat only a block away. He figured Shotty Dread wouldn't risk his freedom knowing this.

Continuing to rant, Shotty Dread surprised him when he said, "You tink' mi don't know about your dealings with the Colombians, mon?"

122

This accusation held validity and caught Scorcher completely off guard.   He thought his tracks were covered.

"Uh Shotty, mi was uh-just trying t....."

Raising his index finger and placing it to his lips, the message was clear as he stopped Scorcher in mid-sentence.

"No reason to explain, mon, everyting' is clear, mi did a little searching. It's been months since we did business togedda, and mi figured you either betrayed me, or ran off with the gal Jasmin, or whatever her name is. Anyway, you know me got the Colombians in mi pocket, and my trusting friend Flacco told me of your dealings with Felipe.   You forget so soon, mi know 'bout everyting' happening in Kingston."

At the mention of Yasmina, Scorcher's heart beat increased.   Was Shotty Dread trying to tell him something? he thought to himself as he tried not to show concern. As far as his survival went, depending on how he played his hand would determine if he would walk out alive. He also knew Shotty Dread didn't travel alone. Glancing around the slightly crowded shop confirmed his suspicions. Two of his Lieutenants sat in the corner, both held bulky-folded newspapers across their laps. Seeing this caused beads of sweat to form over his brow. Nervously, he glanced at his watch. The time was now 7:15 P.M., and he hoped things worked out like he'd planned.

Before he left for the meeting, his concerns were the safety of Yasmina. He knew she was obstinate and didn't want to leave without him, but if he could assure her safety, he'd be able to work things out better. Killing as much time as possible, he wanted her to take a cab if he didn't arrive back home at a specific time. This would assure her safety. Seeing the time, he prayed that she listened.

****

"Damn, what's taking him so long?" Yasmina paced around the huge living room.

For the past couple of hours, she'd called his cell phone over and over again. Her heart wouldn't feel right leaving without him again, that's why she chose to wait. There were things she neglected to tell him, and she figured if he heard them in person, she'd be able to rest easier. However, time was becoming a factor. After racking her brains, she finally dialed another number. Then a thought came to her. Their belongings were already en route to Miami and someone had to be there to claim them. If not, everything would be taken to a holding facility and it would take weeks to get it. Sitting on the ledge of the window, she waited for someone to answer.

"Hey girl, it's Yasmina."

"I know your damn voice, what's up?" Selena jovially stated. "It's about time you called somebody. You had a sista worried the last time we talked."

"Look, I don't have a lot of time to talk, but, can you pick me up from the airport tonight? My flight will be landing at eleven."

"No problem. I was about to kick this limp dick-nigga out of my Condo anyway. I was in need of some dick in a bad way, and this fool can't even get it up. Remember the guy I told you about, the one that works with me. This frontin' ass nigga walks around everyday like his shit don't stink; flirting with me all the time. I finally invited his sorry ass over, and this is what I get, disappointment. Then he had the nerves to say, "I don't understand what's happening, this has never happened." Puhleeze!" She laughed, obviously upset.

Listening to her friend rant and rave, Yasmina didn't hear nor see the minivan approach. The honk of the horn got her attention. Seeing the nappy dread open up the trunk, she grabbed the closest thing to her. A Pen. Grabbing a piece of paper, she hurried and scribbled a note.

BABY, i TRULY HOPE EVERYTHING WENT WELL AT YOUR MEETING. i CAN NO LONGER WAIT, MY CAB HAS ARRIVED. AS MUCH AS i DIDN'T WANT YOU TO GO, i REALIZE IT WAS SOMETHING YOU HAD TO DO FOR YOURSELF. THERE ARE A LOT OF THINGS i DIDN'T GET TO TELL YOU, AND i WISH i HAD. i LOVE YOU WITH ALL MY HEART AND HOPE YOU COME HOME TO ME AND YOUR BABY.

i LOVE YOU, YASMINA

****

"Mr. Rose, we finally meet huh?" Chief Agent Sculea sarcastically said. A few seconds past, then he spoke again.

125

"The last time anyone heard anything from you was what, about eight months ago," his voice came across very imperious.

Cuffed to the chair, Jaheim silently cursed himself, how could he be so stupid to let a piece of pussy trap him? He knew he was on the run, and if caught by the Feds again, it would be his ass. Eight months had passed since he reported anything concrete on Yasmina or Scorcher. The day he wore the wire while talking to Yasmina at the pier, he knew he had come on too aggressively. The way she answered him told him that he was found out. Knowing that Scorcher had a lot of power, he felt the Feds wouldn't be able to protect him, and sitting in some jail cell wasn't an option. However, when his name was leaked over the newspapers, he knew he didn't stand a chance. The only thing left to do was run.

"Mr. Rose, or can I call you Jaheim?" the chief teased. "Yeah, we'll go with Jaheim. Anyway, we have a recorded conversation of you and Yasmina. If I'm correct, you were trying to find out when the next shipment was coming. What happened with that?"

Jaheim sat with his head held low. He knew he was finished. But yet, these people continued to degrade him while trying to drag any information they could get, then they were going to throw him to the wolves. Why should he help them out? He thought to himself.

"Let me rearrange the question," the chief chimed in again. "Why did you evade my agents for eight months? We had to catch you, oppose to you reporting to us like you agreed to do."

"Uh, I wasn't evading you sir. I lost contact with Scorcher and Yasmina. I think they got whiff of what happened through the news. Your agents promised me that they wouldn't let the news leak it. I knew I had to lay low and wait for them to resurface," Jaheim rambled, hoping he bought another day on the streets.

"Well, agent Vincent and Wallace aren't on your case any more. I took it. We have you on a hundred kilos and you haven't delivered anything to us, nil. You left Los Angeles in hopes of never seeing us again, and I don't like it. I think we should go ahead and send you up the river, maybe Lom Poc or Pelican Bay will take a big kingpin such as yourself, you'll be a star!" He held a cold gaze in his eyes.

Not liking the sound of things, Jaheim spoke.

"I think if you give me a little more time, I can come up with someone who will lead us straight to Scorcher. This person I'm talking about is his right hand man," he used his trump card.

While in the holding cell, he wondered why did he ever get involved with that lying ass girl. For the past six months, he'd been working at a Rubber Tree Plant, using an alias, the job wasn't earning him hundreds of thousand like the drug game did, but at least he was free. Living in Oakland didn't afford many opportunities for him to see Rhonda, and he missed her. Every time they talked, she would beg him to come home. In one particular conversation, she told him she was seven months pregnant with his baby, he knew he'd slept with her before going on the run, and to hear this excited him. Falling for the okey-doke, he hopped a Greyhound Bus and headed for the city of Angels.

The city bus made its next stop on 83rd and Rosecrans. Getting off, Jaheim walked in a fast pace towards his destination. Thinking he was unrecognizable, he wore a fitted ball cap pulled low over his braids. Before going on the run, his head was bald.

Walking to the door, he glanced in all directions to make sure he wasn't seen, and then knocked.

"You stinking bitch!" he yelled. "You drag me all the way down this hot muthafucka and your silly ass ain't pregnant."

Trying to get a word in, she said, "Baby I miss you. I know if I would've said anything other than that, you wouldn't have come. "Tears fell from her frightened eyes.

SMACK! Came the sound as his hand forcefully touched the side of her face.

"I'm sorry, I'm sorry," she cried as she cowered from the blows. While this sad display of affection was going on, the occupants in the black van across the street prepared themselves.

"All units, you have a green light," the domineering voice of Chief Agent Sculea said over the radio.

The van and twenty agents emerged out of nowhere. Jaheim turned around to find every kind of gun possible aimed at him. He was caught again.

"We got this piece of shit this time," an agent retorted. "Jaheim, my man, long time no see. I bet you hate you showed your ugly face around these parts, huh?" the chief continued to taunt.

****

Getting up and slowly walking to the door of the café, Scorcher figured his life was about to end. He knew how Shotty Dread played the game, but it was a chance he had to take. Knowing the Lieutenants would follow suit, he was sure to take deliberate steps, hoping that a gunshot in the back wasn't soon to follow.

Reaching for the door handle, a brief glance at his watch saved him. From across the street, atop a building, a sniper beaded in on him and released a shot from his rifle. That brief second of checking his watch saved his life. He heard clink! as the glass shattered into different pieces. Even though the bullet didn't find its target, the sharks caused small abrasions across his hands. From behind, Shotty Dread thought the mission was accomplished until he saw Scorcher duck low and bolt towards the street. A fast moving minivan swept him inside its sliding doors and disappeared around the corner.

Before arriving at the Café Shop, Scorcher called a meeting with his team. He knew a getaway plan needed to be devised. Telling his men to keep an ear out for the buzzing sound of their watches, the plan was followed correctly.

After making it to the door, he glanced at his watch to make sure he gave Yasmina enough time to leave. Everything had to happen with calculated precision. Now that he was safely out of Shotty Dread's reach, he went to phase two.

"You have the boat ready?" Scorcher asked his friend.

"Si amigo."

He made it back to his house within twenty minutes. Knowing it wouldn't be long before Shotty Dread arrived, he gathered the necessities he needed. $250,000 dollars and the codes to the Off Shore Accounts. While in the midst of rounding things up, his attention was averted to something. Yasmina. Picking the not e off the table, he began reading. He let out a big sigh of relief, as he knew he would be with her and his baby soon.

When he got to the beach, he donned his gear. For his plan to work, he had to make a quick identity change. So while the Lobster Boat was underway, he went through the process. Shotty Dread had too many contacts all over Kingston, so the airport couldn't be used. Sailing across the choppy waters, Flacco navigated towards Montego Bay. He still harbored resentment towards Shotty Dread for embarrassing him and his associates the night Poncho was killed.

The trip across the bay wasn't free, as nothing was in the drug game.

Stepping off the boat dressed in a freshly pressed Armani Suit, Alligator Shoes, and a briefcase to match, scorcher presented the I.D. Card with the name Anthony Love on it to the lady at the check-in desk. His head shaven bald, he departed from Sangster International Airport, heading for Miami.

****

"You're home for good?" Selena asked excitedly.

"Yeah, but I'm not gong to let Grandma know yet. I want it to be a surprise," Yasmina answered, but the entire time her thoughts were on Scorcher.

"Damn! This house is huge. When did you guys get this?" She admired the Victorian Style Home with its marble floors and five bedrooms.

"Scorcher got it from one of his realtor friends. A hook up he says," Yasmina replied.

"I'm too jealous. Y'all living like stars out here on coconut Groves. For someone to have the world handed to her, you don't sound too excited." Selena picked up the fact that sadness shrouded her best friend.

After Yasmina explained what was going on, Selena embraced her with a hug. She told her not to worry herself. From what she knew of Scorcher, he would come out of this situation unscathed. Yasmina wished these words were true. She knew all too well about how dangerous Shotty Dread was, and the thought left a bad feeling over her.

While they straightened the few things that were already in the home, Yasmina was interrupted when her cell phone rang. Exhausted and tired from a long day, she was reluctant to answer it, but thought maybe it was Scorcher. Deep down inside, she knew she was wishing upon a star.

"Hello, Yasmina speaking."

Click, the phone went dead in her ear.

14

"In God we trust"

"Ms. Adams, we have you where we want you," Agent Vincent was precise and to the point. "This is some heavy shit you've gotten yourself into. If you must know, conspiracy alone carries up to twenty years, but murder... Now that was a whole different ball game."

Stacey sat uninterested in what the agent had to say, until the word murder sounded in her eardrums. She then looked up as he continued, "Your prints were found at the crime scene of those two fellas killed during bike week. I think that was around May. Is there anything you would like to tell us about that? Any information or insight that leads to a break in this case will help you. I promise."

This was getting too heavy for her, she thought as she listened to the two men throw more and more incriminating evidence at her. Before this new discovery of murder, she had thought hard about riding the time out for the four kilos. Talking to different people on her tier, a swell as her lawyer, she found out that she'd only have to do five years for the drugs. She had a plan. Hearing this, she knew she was in over her head. How did they link her to murder?" She thought as tears rolled down her cheeks. "I want my Lawyer."

"Have it your way Ms. Adams, but you're definitely facing the death penalty now. Save yourself, I'm quite sure whoever you're trying to protect would do the same." Agent Vincent dropped a card on the table with his name on it, then walked out.

When the agents left, she was escorted back to her cell. This time she was distraught. The situation was at a deeper level, and she really was confused now. Walking through population, she kept her head cast to the floor. The sounds of inmates' talking, hollering, and playing games, was drowned out by her deep thoughts. She wished she never crossed Yasmina. If situations were different, Yasmina wouldn't hesitate to come get her, but they weren't.

"Stacey, what's wrong?" the celly named, Angel Santiago asked.

"Shit, what's not wrong," she commented. "These mothers are trying to put a murder on me." She acted as if she couldn't believe it.

"Man that's deep. Are your girls gonna bail you out if they give you a bond?"

"Stacey didn't know how to answer. When she and Angel talked about what landed them in jail, she didn't divulge her betrayal against the PLATINUM CHICKS. With murder, she knew receiving a bond was zero to none. With her mind in shambles, she told her about the money and the forty-six bricks she had stashed. The only problem was getting out.

For twenty minutes, angel listened intently. Not one word missed. After helping relieve some to Stacey's tension, she headed to the TV room. Now as Stacey sat alone, she stared at the card given to her by agent Vincent. Seconds later, she was at the phone dialing him up. After talking, she called her lawyer and set a meeting, and then went to watch the rest of "Days of Our Lives."

"Latoya, what the fuck are you doing?" Yasmina was shocked seeing the gun pointing directly at her head.

She had just opened the safe and began counting her money, when she heard someone behind her. The look in Latoya's eyes told her that there was no room for negotiating. The desert eagle was cocked and ready.

"Yas, I can't wait around and let the Feds just pick me up. My money ain't as long as yours, and you're sitting here acting like shit is gravy. You know Stacey's down there spilling her guts about everything, the drugs and the murders. I'll be damn if I wait for them to come get me."

Yasmina knew she needed to approach the situation delicately. Her gun was on the other side of the room and Latoya was a loose cannon waiting to explode.

"Latoya, calm down. I know you're worried but we can h....."

"Bitch, just give me the money so I won't have to hurt you," she tilted the gun sideways. "You won't miss this little bit. I know you have millions more back in Jamaica."

After hearing this, Yasmina's stomach began to cramp. Only if Latoya knew; she'd just fled Jamaica. She couldn't understand why she was doing this, as she looked up at her. Since they'd been hustling together, she knew each girl had made at least three-hundred grand a piece. So why take hers?

After filling the black-duffle bag, Latoya made sure there wasn't anymore stashed in other places. She then guided Yasmina into the living room closet and locked it. After five minutes. She could hear the door slam shut. Hoping the coast was clear, she pushed the door, but to no avail. It was bombarded and held by the sectional couch. Her only choice was to wait until

Damita made it back. Then a thought came to her. Was Damita in on it also?

While locked in the closet with no way to escape, Latoya embarked on a journey of her own, she jumped into her rental Expedition and barreled it, heading towards the Billy Graham Parkway. She was leaving behind Charlotte, and what she had once known as the PLATINUM CHICKS. Too much drama was unfolding, and her mind was in an irrational state. She felt bad about what she'd done to Yasmina, but her situation had gone from okay to disastrous overnight.

For years, Latoya's mother's health had been on a drastic decline. With no family backing before Yasmina came into the picture, she'd been struggling to provide care for her at home. Working odd jobs and hustling on the side was getting them by, but medication was putting a big strain on both of them. When Yasmina came into the picture, things got better. Latoya was able to find a nursing home that treated patients diagnosed with Alzheimer's disease. With the rising cost of maintenance care, Latoya was now barely getting by again.

With what Latoya had stashed, she easily could've paid the bill up for another year, but she was broke, and with this, came desperation. Her problems, which were minute, turned into something serious when she met Kiana. Kiana was one of the groupie chicks from CJ's. The one she was seen buck naked with by Yasmina and Damita. Since that night, the two had been seeing each other constantly. And Damita was beginning to let her guards down too much. Making runs, Kiana was there, during drop-offs, she was there also. One particular day after being on the grind, Latoya placed a call.

"Hey babe, what's up?"

"You," responded Kiana in her playful-seductive voice. "I miss you and can't wait to give you what I have for you."

Hearing this blew Latoya's mind. Sex with Kiana was fascinating to her. It's like she possessed something that the other women Latoya had slept with didn't. She knew how to press Latoya's buttons and to make her submit. And she loved this. Whole driving to the rooming house where Kiana lived, her thoughts were on the surprise she had coming for her. When Kiana stepped into the SUV, Latoya was all over her. After a quick series of foreplay, the two sped off. While driving, Latoya reached into the back seat, grabbed the duffle bag, and dropped it onto her lap.

"$50,000 dollars, Damn girl, you ballin' like a muthafucka," she stroked Latoya's ego. She'd been doing it ever since the first time Latoya took her to her stash spot.

"Just a lil' somethin' – somethin'."

Latoya was full of herself.

"Girl, you just put $42,000 in there last week, I know you gotta be sitting pretty," said Kiana.

Looking straight ahead and bobbing her head to the music Latoya said, "I'm ai'ight. I have enough to where I can do what I want to, and not worry about anything."

Kiana sat silent taking in everything being said. Her life hadn't been peaches & cream, and a come up was long overdue. Leaving Philadelphia six months ago, she chose Charlotte as her new home, a safe haven for her. Needing to flee her troubles, a friend told her about how fast Charlotte was growing, this presented opportunity. With her profession as a stripper, providing a sister way of life would be easy. However, strip clubs in Charlotte weren't making nearly as much money for her as the ones back home in Philly. Back in Philly, she made money by delivering cocaine for her boss on the side. After getting robbed for two kilos; a cleverly set up plan devised by her boss, she had no choice but to flee the city. This came about when she threatened to inform his wife of the affair. It was a ploy on her part to swindle money from him, but her plan backfired. Now, she'd started a new life in Charlotte and this presented new opportunities.

Parking the SUV and walking into the storage unit, Latoya opened up the huge black footlocker, and started stacking money atop of the cash that was already neatly arranged.

"Damn!" exclaimed Kiana. "Girl, you trust me to see all that money? For all you know, I could be a serial rapist," she chuckled as she probed Latoya's breast and kissed her neck.

"Don't worry, I have a trusted friend named Desert Eagle. He's a Bounty Hunter. If something happens to my cash, I know where to find you," Latoya flashed the big gun, showing a grin on her face.

Twenty minutes later, they pulled into the parking lot of the Sheraton. The only thing on Latoya's mind was what Kiana had said earlier. She wanted to taste the bald thing with a split in the center, surrounded by two-juicy lips, and had strawberries and whip cream for toppings. Breaking out the weed and the bottle of Hennessey she'd purchased earlier that day, the two drank, smoked and sexed each other all night. Adding a game of strip poker to the tenure, Latoya went passed her limits. After Kiana sucked her toes, ate her pussy, and sexed her good with a dildo, she looked on as an intoxicated Latoya soundly slept, snoring. Shaking the bed, dangling the keys, and even smacking her in the face, didn't get a reaction out of Latoya. Seizing the opportunity, she called a cab. Within ten minutes, the cab pulled in front of the hotel and Kiana hopped in. After having the driver help her wrestle the big black footlocker into the trunk, she tipped him twenty dollars, and they sped away from the storage unit. The only sign left to Kiana's presence in Latoya's room was a note that read:

"Last night was the best time I ever had with you. In the beginning, you fucked the shit out of me and I enjoyed every bit of it. In return, I fucked the shit out of you, so we both got what we wanted. In the future, be wary of who you expose your hands to. Let this be a lesson learned."
Kiana

"Fuck!" Latoya cursed as she walked around pulling her hair. "How could I be so stupid."

Waking up to an agonizing headache and hangover, Latoya found that Kiana wasn't anywhere in the room. After finding the note, she became enraged. Speeding over to the storage unit, she knew to expect the worst when she saw the combination lock barely hanging from the door. Walking into the empty unit, the only thing she found was a twenty-dollar bill, laying in the middle of the floor.

This, she couldn't understand. For the past few weeks, she'd treated Kiana to everything; dinner at the nicest restaurants, clothes, and money when she had slow nights stripping at the Gold Nugget. They even made plans to move in together. With this happening and the situation of her mother, Latoya had a choice to make. She could either run with what she made off this last run with Yasmina, which wouldn't be enough, or she could resort to other measures. These things really plagued her as she thought of what to do. She knew she could ask Yasmina for a lookout, but she didn't feel like being chastised. Then there were the Feds.

Now that she'd made her choice, she drove down the highway attempting to escape the clutches of the Feds before it was too late. Looking in her rearview, she could've sworn that white van had been following her since she pulled out the parking lot of the Condo. She made it to the next exit and got off. She wanted to see if the van would do the same. And it did. An Amoco Gas Station was to her right, so she pulled the big Expedition into it. Knowing that things were going to get hectic, she made sure her Desert Eagle was cocked and loaded. 'There is no way she'd be taken alive,' she thought as she nervously fidgeted the gun. Pulling beside a gas pump, she waited.

Seconds after she stopped, the white van pulled up; stopping in front of a telephone booth. While trying to figure her moves, the two agents sat watching. They were well aware that she was on to them. Her eyes gave her away through the rearview mirror. While all attention was given to the agents in back of her, she wasn't aware of the pedestrians and the blue Ford Taurus that pulled directly in front of her. She was blocked in. Seeing the van slowly creep towards her with both doors open, then noticing her getaway path blocked by the blue car, she flipped. Shoving the door open, she stepped out with the Desert Eagle in hand; only to hear, "Freeze, F.B.I."

It was being yelled from both agents as they flashed badges and pointed guns. At that very moment, she started squeezing off round after round. The huge gun exploded; seeming to deafen anyone in the vicinity, and people screamed, scrambled, and dove for cover as the cannon roared. Today wasn't a good day for her to go to jail, so she did everything in her power to keep that from happening, the way she was angled between the door and inside the SUV left Latoya exposed to the oncoming flurry of bullets that were being fired by the two agents.   However, the devastating impact of the Desert Eagle hitting the van, worked to her benefit. The agents had to cower and slightly back off. The onslaught of the bullets were too much. Just as one of the agents fell to the ground, Latoya's body viciously jerked forward. From behind, a bullet slammed into her back, causing her to lose balance and pitch forward.

The gun, now in unsteady hands, still sprayed wildly, hitting everything under the shed of a gas station. One bullet ricocheted and hit a pump, causing a loud explosion.   Not able to flee because of her wounded state, Latoya desperately fanned; trying to put out the fire that the pumps doused on her.   Amidst a horrifying scream and bullets still flying out of her gun, flurries of money fell from the sky. It was minutes later, and minutes too late before the fire department arrived. When everything settled, she lay dead, burnt to a crisp, as many burnt dead-presidents covered the debris filled ground around her.

****

"Oh shit!" Damita exclaimed in shock. "Yasmina, Yasmina, come mere'." Yasmina ran into the living room wondering what could have Damita so excited. Whole listening to a TV reporter talk about a deadly shootout, Yasmina stood wide eyed, mouth open, and shocked.

"Oh shit!," she cursed, not believing what she was hearing, the reporter went on to say, "Agents from the F.B.I. had a shootout with a fugitive-female by the name of Latoya Hicks. Latoya Hicks was wanted for Conspiracy to Traffic Drugs across State lines, and possible murder. A bloody shootout left one dead, Latoya Hicks and one injured – Agent Mark Wallace. An undisclosed amount of money was recovered, but the majority of it was burnt to a crisp. We summed it to be in the amount of $300,000 dollars at the present time. More news at ten o'clock."

Both Yasmina and Damita sat stunned. The seriousness of their situation was becoming clearer by the second. They knew if the Feds wanted Latoya for murder, they were being sought as well. And that meant, Stacey was talking. There was only one thing left to do. Yasmina went her way, and Damita went hers.

15

"The Hit"

Murray pulled into the parking lot of the Club Rolex around 11:00 P.M. His metallic-silver Rang Rover stood out in the dimly lit parking lot as the twilights from the moon and stars made the 22-inch chrome wheels shimmer. Also, Tupac soothed his ears rapping the lyrics of "All Eyes On Me."

After entering the club, he was rushed by employees and customers alike. The distinguished gentleman he is, he held good rapport throughout the establishment. This came from spending tons of money as a patron, and making even more outside of it. As the waitress wearing the two-piece skimpy outfit waltzed over, he made himself comfortable. Placing a bucket of Dom Perignon, along with a wine flute on the table, she said, "Compliments of the house," then walked away smiling. This happened often, and before the night was over, each female working in the club would receive at least $500 dollars from him. Tonight wouldn't be any different.

No sooner than he finished pouring himself a drink, two-almond complexion twins made their way over to his table. The show began. After making his night a little more pleasurable, he prepared to leave. Over the years, and especially for ballers, the strip club served as a prerequisite. You could unwind and receive a little pre-foreplay, then go home fully stimulated and ready for your woman. This proved to be one of those nights.   Back at home, Murray's girlfriend, Felicia, awaited his arrival. Hours earlier, she'd flown in from their vacation home in Orlando. It was his hideaway when he needed to disappear from everything. After having his testosterone level boosted, he headed for the door, but was totally thrown off guard by someone.

"What's up man?" Jaheim placed a hand on his arm stopping him. "I thought that was you."

"Yo dawg, what up?" Murray held a serious expression on his face. "I thought you'd be out in the left coast somewhere. What brings you to these parts?"

"I was in town for some business and figured I'd look you up. I knew I could find you here. I remember the last time we were here, we balled like a muthafucka!"

Murray made a mental note to never come back to this spot. At least while Jaheim was still breathing. He couldn't believe the gall of him, coming up to him like everything was cool. Deep down inside, he knew he was up to no good, and it had everything to do with this supposedly business he was into.

"Hey, I gotta bounce. Got this hottie waiting for me back at the crib, if you know what I mean," Murray tried cutting the conversation short.

"Hey, hold up! Before you go, let me get some digits to reach you at. I need to talk some business with you," Jaheim shifted nervously on his feet.

"Check this out, jot your digits down on a piece of paper, and I'll give you a call tomorrow. How 'bout that?"

After the brief conversation, Murray walked out the door fuming. He knew Jaheim was wired, and couldn't wait to let Scorcher in on what happened.

Scorcher and Yasmina had just finished making love, and were laying cuddled together discussing what had happened with Latoya.   The cell phone ringing interrupted them.

"Hold up!" he held a hand out in gesture. "Yo, he answered.

"What's up my man, I hope I'm not disturbing anything too important. But you're going to want to hear this. Guess who I saw at the Rolex?" said Murray.

Yasmina, not eavesdropping, but interested in the body gestures and facial expressions Scorcher made, couldn't wait until he told her what was going on. She knew something was going down. As fast as he could, Scorcher explained everything to her. He packed a duffle bag with weapons, went into the basement and grabbed some other items, and left. He and Murray went on a mission.

The next morning with nothing to do, Yasmina and Scorcher sat on the bed indecisive about what was going to fill their afternoon. To her, they still didn't seem to find the time to talk about important things. Her situation about Stacey or the baby. Even though he knew, not once since making it safely to Miami did he act as if he was the happiest person in the world. And this bothered her tremendously. Did he really want to have a child? Did she add more pressure on him, knowing how hectic things were for the both of them? All kinds of thoughts consumed her. Feeling that catching a little fresh air would help, she got up and got dressed.

She drove down Brickle Avenue, and passed by the Viscaya Palace and on to twenty-six road; she could see the Shark announcing the Miami Sea Aquarium in the distance. Turning left and then a sharp right, she

144

headed straight towards I-95. In the next couple of minutes, the downtown skyline of Miami could be seen like it had just protruded upward through the earth. Pulling into her grandmother's driveway, Yasmina noticed that the house looked dark and desolate. This was unusual. Normally, if the car was parked in the driveway, the door and windows would be opened. Her grandmother loved to soak up the sun. Yasmina found this strange, and nervousness began to shadow her. After opening the door with her key, she slowly made her way into the stale-smelling home; peering cautiously around the dark interior.

"Grandma!" she yelled, not seeing her. "Uh, what are you doing sitting in the dark. The TV's off, windows are shut, and the door. What's wrong?

"Mi thought mi seen someone sneaking around the yard, a couple days before mi received a phone call from Western Union, they wanted to verify that mi had been receiving money from you. Mi tell them no," she held a frightened look upon her face.

Hearing the words her grandmother spoke caused chills to run down Yasmina's spine. She knew the feds were on to her. Why would Western Union go to such lengths, they had all the information they needed. Standing still in the darkness, she tried to rationalize and come up with something. They were trying to pinpoint a money trail.

"Grandma, I just bought a home in Coconut Groves and I want you to move in with us. It's big enough, besides, I don't want you staying here all by yourself. This is a dangerous neighborhood."

"Babygirl, mi is wise enough to know when trouble's brewing. Get out before it's too late. Mi didn't raise you like this, mi thought me raised you better," her eyes held a tint of sadness.

Speechless, Yasmina had to turn away. She couldn't bear to look her grandmother in the eyes. The truth hurt. But how did she know?" thought Yasmina. Thinking back to everything that'd happened within the last year, she tried once more to convince her grandmother. Her attempts proved futile.

Rosa wasn't about to let anyone nor any kind of trouble run her away from her home. There was too much blood, sweat, and tears involved, and Yasmina had no idea of the lengths of humility suffered so that she would have a place to call home, a place of her own. Thinking back to the 60's and coming from Jamaica, arriving in Miami, she didn't have a pot to piss in or a window to throw it out of. Times were hard and she had to live in a refugee camp until she was cleared to be free. This meant, sleeping beside people who were doomed to die because of some kind of life threatening disease, eating the slop that the place provide, and dealing with perverted animals who achieved sexual gratification by raping others, men or women.

The following weeks after being cleared to leave, she slept on the streets. Having no home, food, or money, she had to fend for her survival. This was all in efforts to provide shelter for her husband and son when they made it to Miami. As degrading as things were, she slept many a nights with strange men. Men she didn't really know. This came from working as a housemaid in some rich peoples' homes. The men she crossed paths with-old and young-got a kick out of sleeping with black women. So even though her sense of pride was breached, she held onto what little dignity she had. She paid her dues with her blood sweat and tears, and her home and all of it's possessions were all the memories she had left to remind her of what could've been. Only if her husband and son would've made it. She wasn't leaving her home.

Giving up, Yasmina was able to talk her grandmother into going furniture shopping with her. Before walking out the door, she cautiously peered through the curtain to make sure they weren't being watched. She knew the Feds were somewhere near.

"Chirp" sound from the walkie-talkies made it obvious that agents were conversing with each other. "I have visual on the subject."

"Copy," replied the voice on the other end.

"Don't make any moves yet, we want to catch her doing something. Hold all positions, I repeat-hold all positions. Have different cars intercepted her wherever she goes, but keep a secure distance so she won't spot us," Agent Shipley spoke into his hand held radio.

"Roger that."

Yasmina and her grandmother drove downtown headed for the Furniture Gallery unaware of anything. Behind them was a convoy of undercovers driving a black Dodge Truck, a white Chevy Corsica, a red Ford Explorer, and a blue Dodge, Neon. Every turn she made, one of them followed. Inside the furniture store, Rosa couldn't believe how careless Yasmina was with money. She spent money like it grew on trees. Well before they were finished shopping, she knew Yasmina had spent every bit of ten-thousand dollars. Then something caught her attention. She glanced over her shoulder, but she didn't find anyone paying attention, so she shunned the thought.

"Grandma what's wrong?" Yasmina glanced in the direction where Rosa was looking.

147

"Nothing's wrong," she didn't want to worry Yasmina. "Mi can't believe how you're blowing money on all that expensive stuff. You have to be frugal. Save some for a rainy day."

"Don't worry, I have some saved up." Only if her grandmother knew.

Right after the words left her mouth, she regretted it. She knew her grandmother didn't approve of Scorcher, and his name was surely to come up next.

"Yasmina, you tink' me crazy and don't notice?"

"What?" she braced herself.

"How many months are you?" the questions was direct.

Yasmina thought she was about to pass out hearing this. How did her grandmother know?

"Grandma, I'm n…."

Interrupting her before she lied, Rosa said, "Gal, you can fool dat' young man, but a wise ol' lady like me is hard to fool," she placed a hand on Yasmina's stomach.

After confessing, they left the furniture store and headed for a restaurant. The red Ford Explorer followed in the distance.

****

"Aye yo, hurry up dawg!" These bitches is gettin' restless," Murray said to Jaheim. "I didn't pay all this money for you to take your time. I'm in room #205 at the Residence Inn.

As gullible as he was, he fell for the bait. He had no inkling of what was in store for him. With the Feds being persistent, and him trying to avoid prison, he was going to any length to seal this deal. Murray was going to be his "get out of jail-free card." Adjusting his clothes, he made sure the wire wasn't visible. Once satisfied, he hopped into the rental Grandprix and headed for the Residence Inn. "Shit, who wouldn't mind getting a piece of ass while putting in a little work," he said to no one in particular as he drove.

Hearing the loud-thumping bass through the hotel room door, he knew this was going to be easier than he thought. What better way to catch a nigga slippin'? get'em drunk and the rest is history. Checking himself one more time, he spoke into his shirt. He wanted to be sure the agents got everything clearly. When the door opened, the music blasted in his eardrums.

"Nigga, I thought you had some bitches up in here." He was pissed after noticing no females around.

"Chill out fool, they're upstairs getting' ready. They almost left because of your slow ass," Murray played his part.

While fixing drinks, Murray was careful to say as less as possible. He knew Jaheim was wired, that's why he kept the music blasting.

"Check this out Dawg, can you turn that music down? I wanna talk some business with you. You know, while the bitches are still upstairs," he yelled over the music.

"My man, we got all night to talk business. What, you in a hurry to make it back to Cali? Besides, you gon' like these bitches I got for you."

After ten minutes had passed, Jaheim began to get restless.

"Damn! What's taking them hoes so long? I been here damn near twenty minutes."

Before Jaheim arrived at the room, Scorcher informed Murray that he was very impatient. And this would make the plan work to their advantage. Reflecting back to a drug deal that went on between him and Jaheim, he knew it was just a matter of time.

When he first started dealing with Jaheim, Scorcher made plans for him to meet at the pier where the Cargo Ship usually docked. The ship was running a few minutes late, Jaheim went ballistic. He started calling Scorcher's phone. Scorcher told him that a crewman had found an oil leak in one of the bilges, and it had to be contained before the ship could enter port. Within an hour's time, Jaheim had phoned him five times. He became so impatient he started using incriminating words like cocaine, drugs, and shipment, unaware of what he was saying. When Scorcher hung the phone up in his ears, this made him worse.

Since it would be nightfall before everything was taken care of, Scorcher told him they'd handle business the next day. That same night as the ship was finally able to enter the port, Scorcher saw Jaheim barreling down the pier in his chromed-out red SC-500 Series Mercedes, music on blast. Since that day, he knew how impatient Jaheim was, and he would play right into their hands.

Still not seeing any women, Jaheim bolted up the stairs. He was tired of waiting. They were holding up important business, and the sooner they were out the way, the quicker he could handle his business. Not hearing any voices as he stood at the door, he turned the knob.

"Bloodclot battyboy!" Scorcher said as he bashed him beside the head with the 10mm Glock.

Without hesitation, Murray ran up and helped drag the limp body into the bathroom. Taping his mouth shut and binding his feet and hands together, they heaved his heavy body into the already half-filled tub of Sulfuric

Acid.   Smoke and putrid scent emanated as his body deposited itself deeper and deeper into the solution.   As the searing and burning of flesh drifted up his nostrils, he slowly came to.   In a daze, once his eyes registered who stood over him, the fear factor kicked in.   It was evident why he was invited to the room.

The look in his eyes told a story of death, his. When Scorcher snatch-opened his shirt, their suspicions were confirmed.   A black wire was taped to his chest. Seconds later, Murray walked in holding two huge containers.   Pouring the substances in with the acid that was already in the tub caused Jaheim to jerk violently. His skin started melting, his face, and his eyes begged for mercy.   The stench was beginning to be too much. Donning respirators, Scorcher and Murray watched as he tried his best to break free of the clutches that bind him. Little by little, his body turned into bone and mush.   As the smoke clouded the place, his once body was hard to distinguish amongst all the gook in the bathtub.

An hour later, only a gel like pulp remained in the tub.   The acid had eaten everything, everything except the wire.   Thoroughly wiping down everything, sure not to leave a single print in the entire room, they gathered what cartilage was left, and threw 'em into a trash bag.

"Can you make out what they're saying?" Agent Vincent asked his partner.

"Who knows, he's probably getting his freak on. That's what the brothers call it." The agents chuckled at the funny comment.

While Jaheim was inside doing his work, the two agents decided to take a break and eat their cold lunch. Since Jaheim was wired, they wouldn't miss too much conversation.   It was being recorded.   They also figured since the room was packed with strippers that no one would be going anywhere anytime soon.

"Wallace, you know these snitches make our jobs a heck of a lot easier. I mean, they sell dope, buy fancy cars, live with their mommas, and when the heat is turned up and they're caught, they tell on each other. Take Stacey for instance….."

"You mean Ms. Adams?" Agent Wallace asked. "The chick that got caught selling the four kilos to Agent Shipley and his partner."

"Yeah, she's the one. Well anyway, turns out that she's not taking this wrap alone. The murder made her change her mind. She's willing to testify, in hopes that we could come to a deal."

"Is that right?" retorted his partner.

"She also said that Yasmina is the ring leader. And, she has a boyfriend named Scorcher," he chuckled. "Where do your people get these outlandish names from? Shaquana, Shaniqua, Mercedes. Christ, that's a car," he purposely berated his partner's ethnicity, but Agent Wallace laughed along with him. Can you see where I'm headed with this?"

Agent Wallace had no clue where this situation was going.

"Our snitch, Jaheim," he let the words linger for a second. "He said, he used to work for Scorcher when we busted him a…."

"Shit, so that means if we get Murray, he can lead us to Scorcher." The agent was excited that he'd discovered the link.

"Hold up, I'm not finished yet. Remember the Spanish chick Angel Santiago? Well, she's Stacey's celly in the county. And it seems that our girl isn't being straight up with us," agent Vincent went on explaining.

After eating, they sat in the back of the van and discussed how big of a case they really had. The one person they needed most was Scorcher. Apparently, he was too smart to show his face. If they had to track him all the way to Jamaica, then he was prepared to do it, Agent Vincent thought to himself while donning his headphones.

While they were busy eating and talking, Murray and Scorcher were making a clean escape right under their noses. Having pictures of both men, there was no way they could leave the hotel without being spotted, thought the agents. However, they weren't prepared for Scorcher or Murray.

"How can someone walk around all day with that much hair on their heads? You would think that dirt and all kinds of bugs lived in something like that. Dreadlocks!" Agent Vincent smirked as he talked to his partner.

"Lets finish this surveillance, don't wanna miss all the action,' his partner replied.

16

"DESTINATION, MIAMI"

The Sunrays glistened off the Aluminum fibers of the DC-10 Airplane as it descended onto the runway. Stepping off, Shotty Dread and his two trusting Lieutenants headed through the terminal. After hailing a cab, they were taken to a hotel where Shotty Dread called some of his contacts and had the necessary weaponry they needed delivered. He was on a mission, and it wouldn't be complete until Scorcher was dead.

Intent on finding their whereabouts, he passed out pictures and an address, as to where Yasmina and Scorcher may be living. With this information, the contacts set out to find the two. That night proved worthless, but bright and early the next morning, a huge break came through. The turn of events would spawn Shotty Dread to react in a deadly rage. Hearing that Scorcher and Yasmina were spotted in a mall, they drove the rental car through the streets of Miami like he was Governor of the State. When he arrived at his destination, he hopped out of the car limping violently as he led the way into the crowed structure. At a phone booth, one of his contacts awaited his arrival.

The entire time Scorcher and Yasmina browsed through the windows in each shop, but in the back of their minds they felt the presence of someone watching them. They both knew the Feds were pursuing them, and figured sooner or later they would move in for the kill. As Scorcher glanced over his shoulder, what he saw made his heart stop. Shotty Dread and three men stood not even forty feet away; all wearing evil grins.

Yasmina, sensing something wrong, turned to look. The second after she saw them, she was being dragged through crowds of men, women and children. The bags she carried were now scattered all over the floor, and they were running for their lives. "If only they could make it outside they would be half of the way back to safety," Scorcher thought.

Desperately breathing hard and running, crossing the vehicle filled and driven parking lot was an obstacle in itself. Pedestrians were scattered about, cars and trucks and even city buses came and went. Seeing the Mercedes only twenty feet away, excitement and happiness shot through Scorcher. He knew with the press of a button on the keyless remote, they'd be homeward bound and safe once again. Yasmina was the first to enter. She made it around the passenger side because the flurry of bullets was turning the driver's side into Swiss cheese. But Scorcher still fought to gain entrance. Proceeding to get his door opened, he was stopped dead in his tracks. A bullet slammed into his spine causing him to fall to his knees. Still in between the opened door, Yasmina grabbed on in attempts at pulling him into the vehicle. In tears, she struggled at the dead weight that stared at her as life slowly began to drain from his eyes. A few seconds later, she could see a handcrafted-cane, followed by an awkward limp, making it's way behind him. Blood slowly dribbled down Scorcher's back. To make matters worse, Shotty Dread took his cane and mangled it deeply into the wound. The barrel of a 9mm pistol was pointed at the back of his head, and that's when Yasmina started screaming. She pleaded and begged earnestly for them to spare his life, but with no feeling of remorse, Shotty Dread ordered his man to fire.

"Shaw'ty! Shaw'ty, wake up, you're dreaming," Scorcher shook Yasmina, trying to wake her out of her nightmare.

Sitting up, her face was wet from an admixture of tears and sweat, and her nightgown was soaked. Trembling, Yasmina couldn't stop crying. Scorcher saw that she was shaken, had no idea why she was crying or what the nightmare was about. All he knew was, it had to be a bad one.

****

"This is strange, don't you think?" Agent Vincent asked his partner, puzzled as to why the hotel room appeared to be unused.

"Are you sure we're in the right room," asked Agent Wallace.

"Yes I'm sure, you idiot. We watched when Jaheim walked in. There, look, 205, that's the room number. Or weren't you paying attention?" He sharply emptied his frustrations on his partner. "Remember the dreadlock Rasta guy that came to the door? It was this room; I'm as sure as a stack of bibles in a church."

"Hey, you don't have to snap on me, I'm on your side, remember? We're the good guys and they're the bad ones."

"Aye, I'm sorry man. I'm just frickin' pissed that we let them slip away right under our noses. We can't afford to blow this one, it'll mean our asses." Agent Vincent thought about what Chief Sculea told him the last time Jaheim slipped away during their watch.

Back in the van, they both sat motionless. Their eyes were peeled on any and everything that moved on the hotel premises. Seeing Jaheim's rental car gave them some hope. They might've gotten hungry or something, Agent Vincent surmised, realizing that it was a chance that they'd let their subjects escape again, he was highly perturbed.

As the grueling hours passed, darkness crept in on the two trite but very anxious agents, and Jaheim never cooperated. Cramped, they both nodded viciously as they waited for any movement on the premises.

"Hey," Agent Vincent nudged his partner, "wake up. It's already 8:30 A.M. How did we let the time slip by on us?" he looked for confirmation.

"Huh, uh-whuh-damn!" Agent Wallace cursed after his eyes adjusted on his watch. "I'm sorry man, I didn't mean to fall asleep," he yawned.

Realizing that they'd wasted an entire day, they were about to head in. Then a thought came to Agent Vincent.

"Hey, go check the dossier at the clerk's office. They should have all the information we need, and while you're doing that, I'll go over the room one more time."

With their jobs on the line, desperation began to set in. There had to be a clue left, something that would acknowledge that they were surveying the right room, thought Agent Vincent as he twisted the knob on the door. Readying his weapon, he shoved the door open quickly, using his weight like a battering ram. What he heard was a piercing scream so loud, it almost caused him to pull the trigger. Crouched on her knees, face to the floor and in tears, was the old white cleaning lady. This caused a rage from deep inside to surface in the face of Agent Vincent. Making his way to where his partner stood in the front office only caused more irritation to his morning. There wasn't anything solid that could lead them to Murray, Scorcher, or Jaheim. The one person that cold be of assistance was missing, and they desperately needed something. While driving back to headquarters, Agent Vincent took a detour.

"Where are you headed now?" asked his partner.

Agent Vincent was in deep thoughts at the time and didn't answer his partner. His mind was on his situation at home. He had two kids, teenagers, and his wife pregnant with his third child. His oldest son Danny was Autistic, and the money he was making was barely keeping his family above water. He couldn't afford to lose his job. His mind was elsewhere. After pulling into the Metro Dade County Jail parking lot, his partner finally figured it out. They were going to chat with Stacey.

****

After a long tedious day of shopping, Yasmina dropped her grandmother off, and went home. Although she pleaded and begged her grandmother to come live with her, it was senseless. She wouldn't budge. Knowing about the Western Union deal and her grandmother seeing someone snooping around, she couldn't relax. The entire drive back across town, she used her rearview mirrors. Later that night after making it home, getting to sleep was a task. Scorcher wasn't anywhere around and this troubled her. Not to mention the fact that she couldn't stop thinking about Shotty Dread. Something told her that he was coming for them.

Thinking back to her college days, Yasmina could remember how every female her age considered themselves baller chicks. This was a status symbol. If your man drove around in the phattest whips, wore the nicest jewelry and clothing, and had money out the anus, you were respected.

Getting a taste of how good the life was, Yasmina became addicted to the good life. That is when she decided to make her mark in the game. It was to become the baddest female in the game since Foxy Brown. Now that she'd accomplished this, she realized that it wasn't all it cut out to be. Recollecting on all the events that's happened since venturing into this underworld, she wondered how she ever became the monster that she was seeing in the mirror. While lying in the bed, head full of thoughts, the questions she asked herself caused tears to slide down her face. "I took the lives of two people," she softly said as she rubbed her swollen stomach. She knew she needed to be free of this life forever, but she was in too deep. There was no turning back.

****

"Thank you very much, Angel, if this information proves to be solid, it'll help you out tremendously," Agent Vincent shook her hand before she walked out the room.

The minute she made it back to her cell, Stacey was called and told she had a visitor. Puzzled, Stacey wondered who could be visiting as she followed the officer down the hall. She made it to the window to the interrogation room, and saw the two agents and wondered what the meaning of the visit was. She'd given them all the information on the PLATINUM CHICKS days before.

"Mrs. Adams, we need some information from you." Agent Vincent was direct and to the point. "Have you ever heard of a guy named Scorcher?"

"Before I answer, I wanna know how this is going to help me," she peered deep into the agents' eyes. "Do I need my lawyer present?"

"Nah, no need for your lawyer, just simple questions we're asking, it'll most definitely help you," Agent Wallace chimed in.

Falling for the Academy Award Winning Act, Stacey started spilling her guts. Not once did the agents mention the conversation they held with her celly, Angel. Their plans were to drain her for every piece of information she knew, then hang her out to dry.

"We want you to know how serious this thing is," Agent Vincent threw a newspaper clipping on the table.

After reading a few lines, Stacey glanced up and saw his arm bandaged, then the reality of reading that Latoya was killed during a gun battle with him sunk in. Visibly distraught, she couldn't stop herself from crying. Even after being escorted back to her cell, she was in a feeble state. Having a friend like Angel to console her and tell her everything would be all right, eased the pain a little.

****

Sitting in the den watching TV, Rosa jumped, startled by a sound she thought she'd heard. She was slightly paranoid from being in the furniture store earlier, and the same sound she had been hearing outside her door for the past couple of days, was back again. Gripping the huge butcher's knife, cradling it like a baby,

160

she sat waiting for the trespassers to violate her abode. Her adrenaline was at it's highest point. Five minutes passed and nothing. No sounds of the door rattling or clogging of shoes through her front lawn. Hoping everything was clear; she slowly stood and cautiously made her way to the curtains. She caught the mailman pulling out of her yard, heading up the block, and then he disappeared around the corner.

Around the same time the following day, the sound could very well be heard again by Rosa. This time, as she baked Creole chicken and herbed rice, she didn't bother worrying herself. She knew it was the mailman making his rounds. The thick spices of lemon, onions, peppers, and mushrooms pasted the kitchen with its tantalizing aroma, and she planned on enjoying this meal. Letting the dish cool down and simmer a bit, she decided to see what mail awaited her in the small metal box hanging outside the door. The second the doorknob turned, "BLAM!" was the sound heard as the force of the men rushing in on her caused her to fall to the floor. Stunned, not able to make out what or who barged into her home unwelcome, she was finally able to focus on the men pointing guns at her.

On the brink of having a heart attack, Rosa couldn't find the strength to move. The blow of the gun hitting her didn't help either; it almost caused her to blackout. Regaining some sort of consciousness, she found herself duct taped, bound and gagged to a chair. As blood trickled down her clothing, a confused look came across her face. "Why is this happening to me? Who are these people in my house pointing guns at me?" These thoughts were rudely interrupted when the short-dark-skinned man with the cane and dreadlocks stood over her.

That precise moment, it all came back to Rosa. He was the man she saw at the furniture store, he was watching hem. Shotty Dread.

"What'tar you doing in my house?" The words were strangles, but clear enough to be heard. "Mi will call t...."

Rosa's words were cut short when a heavy hand stung her face from a vicious slap. Fear absorbed her and she figured it was best to remain silent. Whatever these men wanted, they clearly didn't mind hurting, or even kill her for it.

Walking around the small room, Shotty Dread made his way over to the stovetop. Lifting the lid and inhaling the aroma of the food, he looked at his men and gestured his approval. Seconds later, he walked back over to Rosa and made his introduction. Rosa couldn't believe what she was hearing, Yasmina's not involved in drugs! How could she owe this man twenty million dollars? Sitting in deep thought, she tried soaking this shocking information up.

Each time Shotty Dread questioned Rosa, he'd end up becoming angrier and angrier. This lady wasn't going to willingly hand Yasmina's whereabouts over, so other methods had to be implemented. Whispering in one of his Lieutenants ears, he ordered her tortured. The savage treatment of slapping, punching, strangling, and threatening wasn't enough to force the information out of Rosa. She steadfastly endured the punishment. When all else failed, Shotty Dread was about to order his men to finish her, but the ringing of the telephone grabbed his attention. Leisurely walking over to it, he glanced down at the caller I.D. "Bingo!" he thought to himself, seeing Yasmina Powell #305-555-2106 flash across the screen.

As the phone continued to ring, he ordered one of his men to hold the receiver to Rosa's ear. Placing the sharp blade of the machete against her throat, he gestured his head for her to speak.

"You tell her ta come over. If you mention that I'm here, mi will kill you dead," Shotty Dread spat in his raspy Jamaican accent.

"Hello," Rosa stifled the word out."

"Grandma, are you alright, you sound sick? I'll stop by a store and get you some medicine, I'm on my way over."

This left Rosa with a big decision to make. She knew that either way things turned out, she was going to die. To let Yasmina suffer along with her would be fruitless. As she sat thinking, she came to a conclusion. There's no way she would let her daughter and granddaughter die at the hands of Shotty Dread. In a calm voice she said, Yasmina, mi want …Shotty Dread is h…..."

The phone was snatched away from her and Shotty Dread's scary voice echoed into Yasmina's eardrum. The words were harsh, and she could feel the danger radiate through the line. Tears streamed down her face as she pleaded for her grandmother's life, but to no avail. A second later, the phone went dead in her ear. She knew it was the last time she'd ever heard her grandmother alive.

****

Bond hearing was scheduled for Thursday October 9 bright and early in the morning. Stacey held big hopes in receiving a bond reduction. That meant going home or following through with her intended plans. But there was a catch; the information she'd given the agents had to prove worthy.

In the courtroom, her lawyer prepped her on how things would proceed. As the U.S. Attorney presented her case to the Magistrate, Stacey listened intently. She was painted as a Drug Kingpin and a murderer, and berated for her place in society. This made her uncomfortable in her seat, and every now and then she'd look to her lawyer for counsel, but seeing the two agents seated in the courtroom eased her consternations. They'd kept their words, and it was only a matter of time and she'd be on her way out the door, she meditated in her mind.

The first thing she planned to do was head over to the storage unit. A little money would be needed to carry out her plans. Moving some of the bricks would put some cash in her pockets. Second, she'd spend a little time with her mother. Since she planned on running, she didn't know how much time would pass before they saw each other again. And last, she needed to find another state or city where she could get her grind on. It was still a lot of money out there and this time she would be the boss. However, her thoughts were rudely interrupted when she heard the Magistrate convey that her bond was denied.

"What the fuck do you mean denied because of new charges?" she blared, staring at the judge then back to her lawyer. "Those two agents told me if I cooperated they'd get me a bond reduction," she pointed towards Agent Vincent and Wallace.

"That is all true and I'm well aware of what was agreed upon Ms. Adams, but there seems to be a new charge against you of Conspiracy to Maintain a Dwelling and Possession of forty-six kilos of Cocaine. They were found in a storage unit and your name was on the lease. Paid up for a year," the Magistrate affirmed from the papers she was reading.

Stacey's lawyer sat looking confused. He had no idea or insight about the new charges. There wasn't much he could do for her in the beginning other than pleading with the judge to grant her life in prison since she'd cooperated, she knew that the death penalty wouldn't be ruled out. After discovering that the information that led to the new findings came from Stacey's cellmate, Angel Santiago, there wasn't anything he could do. He did inform her that in order to proceed as her lawyer, the price would rise drastically.

To say that she was enraged is an understatement. She became crazed; cursing the Magistrate, spitting at the two agents, and ramming her head into anything near her. After being hogtied, she was driven back to the county where she was led to her pod. Upon walking in, the bunk that held her celly's linen was stripped bare. She was gone and not one trace of her presence was left.

17

"DANGEROUS GROUNDS"

"Did you hear what just came across the scanner?" Agent Vincent asked his partner, after stepping out of the courthouse.

"No shit, that's the place Agent Shipley was staking out a few days ago. Yvette, Yamin, or whatever her name is, that's where her grandmother lives." Agent Wallace sounded surprised.

"I guess we don't have to worry about tracking the money through Western Union, huh?" Agent Vincent smirked. "The old lady's dead."

The validity to the situation was taking on a new meaning for the agent as he figured out his next move. He knew this was bigger than drugs; someone was out for vengeance, but why? And who? Agent Vincent pondered his questioning. Innocent people were being killed and it was behind Yasmina and Scorcher. They had to react fast, because the bloodshed wasn't going to stop until both of them were dead.

Once they made it to the scene, they couldn't believe their eyes. Following the lead Detective as he guided them around the gruesome scene, the smell of freshly cooked food was very apparent. Blood was everywhere, and this caused Agent Wallace to dry heave. The body of Rosa was placed in a chair duct taped, and her throat was slashed from ear to ear. Upon further viewing, they found a foot, severed at the ankle, lying beside the chair. A note was attached to her chest – held by a knife that said, "**YOU CAN RUN, BUT YOU CAN'T HIDE. MI WILL KILL ANY AND EVERYTING' IN MI PATH TO GET YOU SCORCHER. BLOODCLOT!**" When the agents read the note, they both stared at each other. They ordered an All Points Bulletin (APB) on Yasmina immediately. They knew that whoever Scorcher was, he had to piss this guy off. With a bloody and cold killer at large, the next place they headed was Yasmina's home in Coconut Groves.

"Team One, you ready?" Agent Vincent made sure he had the entire home covered. An end needed to be put to this murdering spree, and bringing both Scorcher and Yasmina in would do the job.
"Roger, Team One ready," a voice responded.
"Team two and three, your positions?"
"Two and three ready," responded another voice.
"Copy that. All teams go, let the dogs loose!" replied Agent Vincent. As the doors of the vans flew open, the only thing moving on the quiet suburban street were a swarm of agents dressed in black. More than twenty FBI Agents carrying HK-MP5 Automatic Machine guns and enough ammunition to start a small war, ran at full speed in attempts to gain entrance into the huge home. Crouched low, and single filed, they made their way to the front door, guns ready. Heaving the huge-heavy steel battering ram, splinters and chunks of wood shattered as the door flew off its hinges. They were inside the house in seconds.

****

167

Yasmina couldn't shake the thought of hearing the fright in her grandmother's voice. The minute Shotty Dread got on the phone, she knew death was certain. It was his way of proving how powerful he was, and making a statement saying that he was above the law. Still crying, she wondered how he found their whereabouts. How did he know where her grandmother lived? The thought of being the cause of her grandmother's death hit her hard. Dialing Scorcher's cell phone, she cried profusely as she explained what had just occurred.

Scorcher was shocked to hear what had happened to her grandmother, but he wasn't all that surprised that Shotty Dread went through great lengths to achieve the things he wanted. Hearing Yasmina say that she was sure she could convince her grandmother to move in with them, he came up with a plan. Knowing Shotty Dread would use the information, he wanted to have him on an even playing field. That way, things would be easier when he attempted to kill him. Now the plans had to change. Yasmina was in danger, so he told her about the escape route.

When they bought their house, Scorcher knew they would need more than one or two ways to flee the Feds. After having his realtor friend show him three homes, the one he decided to purchase now was perfect. Having an intersection at both ends of the street was good, but the thick wooded area behind the house was even better. It held a path that led to a dirt road, and the road led to the old Highway 75.

Since Shotty Dread was hot on their trails, he knew the Feds weren't too far behind. He desperately begged and urged Yasmina to gather what little things she could of personal value and leave. Following the direction, she dizzily stumbled into the house. Making it inside her bedroom closet, she started looking for important things, while her mind reflected back to when she was at the University of Miami.

Her freshmen year, her grandmother called her into her room one day. Sitting on the edge of the bed, she held a shoebox. After talking for a while, she pulled out a bag that contained a bunch of old photos. On the picture, Yasmina's mother, father, Rosa, and she were seated around a small room. Her grandmother gave her this picture after telling her she'd been saving the only memories she had of her family. Now that Yasmina held it in her hands, tears fell from her eyes. Knowing that time was of the essence, she grabbed her purse, picture in hand, and made her way out of the back door. Trudging through the thick weeds, she made it deep into the desolate woods. The silence was eerie and spooked her a little. Scorcher promised he'd be waiting at the dirt road, so she tried her best to make it through. Soon, a light could be seen and it brought hope to her spirit.

Murray and Scorcher were a quarter of a mile away from the intended spot. Their minds were just a messed up as Yasmina's, but they were going to get her. Scorcher hadn't uttered one word since his conversation with her. He felt bad about killing her parents and getting her grandmother killed. If she found this out, she surely would leave him. As the car came to a stop, they both waited to see when she would appear. The entire wooded area was only a five minute walk through, and they wondered what was taking so long. Catching a glimpse of what appeared to be a body lying on the ground, they stared at each other. For a second, it appeared to disappear. Walking through the weeds, they headed in the direction of it. A few feet away, Scorcher saw why the figure appeared and disappeared. The high weeds practically covered Yasmina's body as she lay passed out.

Unconscious, she lay face down; dirt, weeds, and splinters of debris covered her body. Though she was unconscious, Scorcher could see the pain and hurt etched on her face. Gently but hurriedly, he lifted her off the ground and carried her back to the car. While attempting to flee before it was too late, he didn't see the photo drop out of her hand. The twenty-minute ride to Ft. Lauderdale was thought-filled and a quiet one. Glancing in the direction of each other, Scorcher and Murray were subliminally thinking the same thoughts. "The Feds were going to have her picture on every TV station across the nation."

When they got to Murray's four-bedroom Georgian home, they helped Yasmina up the stairs and into a bedroom.

"Felicia, run some warm water and clean her up please," Murray ordered. He eyed Yasmina with a sorrowful gaze. "Give her some clothes, too."

Looking at the terribly distraught, dirty, and haggard girl, Felicia asked,

"What happened to her? Looks like she's been through hell."

"Just do what I said," snapped Murray. He didn't like seeing Yasmina in this state either.

Felicia was still in town visiting with Murray. She had a couple more days before gong back to Orlando, and the weekend was supposed to be a quiet one spent together. As she wiped the dirt and grass away from Yasmina's face, she knew the weekend was going to be everything but that. In the other room, Scorcher and Murray talked about their next move. They knew

Shotty Dread had to be dealt with, or he'd chase them all over the United States. Then there were the Feds.

Knowing that the next few days, weeks, or even months would be filled trying to hunt Shotty Dread down, Scorcher relayed information about the codes to the Offshore Accounts to Murray, and he was to give all the information to Yasmina. Shaking his best friend's hand, Scorcher walked into the bedroom where Yasmina lay sleeping like a baby. He could see a calm over her face that he hadn't seen since her college days. Brushing her hair to the side, he placed a soft kiss to her forehead then to her lips. Lifting her shirt, he placed his head against her slightly swollen belly, then kissed the baby goodbye. Not knowing if he'd ever see her again, he walked out the door with one thing in mind, to kill Shotty Dread.

****

Yasmina's cell phone rang continuously. Both Damita and Selena tried phoning after seeing her picture broadcast over the television. Selena was in the middle of cooking dinner when the news flashed about Rosa being murdered. Then seconds later, Yasmina's picture came across the screen. This caused her to worry. To hear the reporter declare that she was wanted for Conspiracy to Distribute and Traffic Drugs, and at the present sought for murder, blew her mind. This couldn't be her best friend that they were talking about! She shook her head in disbelief. After leaving numerous messages on her voicemail, she deiced to wait for Yasmina to call her back. She knew that sooner or later she'd hear from her.

Over the next two days, Selena didn't receive a call. She began to worry because it was the day of Rosa's Funeral. Figuring Yasmina would show up there, she managed to get dressed and headed out. When she arrived at the cemetery, she was shocked to find that there was hardly anyone there. A few people that knew Rosa were in attendance. Federal Agents were placed here and there and concealing their identities weren't something they tried to do. FBI was written all over their jackets. Upon all the mourners, Selena expected to see Yasmina somewhere, but didn't. But someone caught her attention.

As the services went on, something felt out of place to Selena. The three men who stood in the distance seemed out of place. It was something about them that didn't quite fit the category of friends of Rosa's. She contemplated as she stared at the short man with a handcrafted cane. He kept looking around like he was trying to find someone.

As the casket was being lowered into the ground, the short man limped over. The Titanium Coffin was just a couple inches above the hole when the man tossed a picture into it. This caused her to be curious. Little did Selena know, it was the same picture that had fallen out of Yasmina's hand when Scorcher lifted her off the ground. She was now marked for death.

****

"Did you hear what those morons did?" Agent Vincent asked his partner.

"What? Who are you talking about?"

172

"The news nitwit!" he held his phone up. He'd just finished talking to his colleagues back at headquarters. "They've blown our covers again. What did you tell them? I hope you told him to say that Yasmina needed to phone the nearest law agency because her life was in danger," he eyed his partner.

"Well I umm, uh, I told them to put an APB out. They asked the reason and I told them that…."

"Jesus, you idiot! Why did you do that? We have priority over what is to be said on television or radio, and they're on a need to know basis. Geesh! There's no way we'll find them now. For all we know, they may be in BUM-FUC-EGYPT by now. I'll tell ya, if we don't lose our jobs over this, I'm finding me a new partner once this case is over," Agent Vincent was raging mad.

Having exhausted all their leads, they headed back to headquarters. The only reason Chief Sculea hadn't been breathing down their necks was because of the murder of Rosa and the connection to Scorcher. However, they had to face the reaper and it wasn't going to be nice.

18

"Watching your Back "

"Girl, what took you so long to call me? Selena was delighted that Yasmina finally called. "Where've you been? I've been trying to reach you for days.

Still sniveling, Yasmina remarked, "I'm sorry, I left my cell phone in the house, I was in a hurry. Do you think your line is secure enough for us to talk?"

"Yea, we're alright."

"Look, I don't know what 's gong on. All I know is that they killed grandma." She started sobbing more. "I didn't go to the fune…."

"Shhh! It's alright, go ahead and cry," Selena tried consoling her friend.

"You don't have to explain anything. I just needed to know that you were safe, and I went to your grandmother's funeral. She'd understand. Look, I rather talk to you in person, you could use a real friend right about now. Where are you?

After providing Selena with the address in Ft. Lauderdale, Yasmina hung up the phone. Her mind was still in shambles, and the thought of Scorcher gone to avenge Shotty Dread made her even more fragile. When she awoke earlier in the morning, she was told that Scorcher had left all of his information about the money he had in different Offshore Accounts. Hearing this frightened her. Why would he abandon her like this? Will he make it back alive to be with her and his child?

All sorts of thoughts filled her head. The only thing to relieve the pain was to ball into the fetal position.

As she anticipated Selena's arrival, a thought occurred to her. What happened to my picture? She frantically searched around the bedroom. Frustration mounting.

Felicia noticed how abrupt Yasmina jumped out the bed, wondered what the problem was. She watched as Yasmina searched under the bed, in the closet, checked her old dirty clothes, and even the bathroom. When she saw the deflated look on her face, she knew whatever Yasmina was looking for, was very dear and precious to her. Not knowing what to do, she left Yasmina to her thoughts.

Shotty Dread made it to Yasmina and Scorcher's home in the Coconut Groves an hour after the federal Agents left. He walked through and he could tell it wasn't long since their departure. The door was busted into pieces and barely hung on the hinges. During his inspection of the home, he was alerted by one of his men; showing him what looked to be a path leading through the woods. Following the path led them to an open field, and that's where they found the picture. It was partially buried between the dirt and weeds. At closer scrutiny, a tennis ankle bracelet with the initials YASMINA etched in it lay not too far.

All of these clues led Shotty Dread to the funeral. And by chance, he hoped someone would lead him right to Scorcher and Yasmina.

****

After hearing the bell ring, Yasmina ran to the door and peered through the tiny peephole. She knew Selena was arriving soon, but deep inside wished it was Scorcher coming home to surprise her. After opening the door, the two girls embraced each other with a deep hug, and the tears of sadness and joy started flowing.

"You made sure you weren't followed, right?" Yasmina took one last look out the door.

"Yeah, I doubled back, then went to the Wal-Mart around the corner. I wanted to make sure," Selena added.

Felicia left the two sitting huddled on the sofa. She could sense the closeness, and at a time like this, she knew they wanted to be alone.

"Yas, what's really going on?"

"Girl, it's a long story, and honestly I'm ashamed to tell you about it."

"C'mon Yas," she looked into Yasmina's eyes, "this is me, your best friend. I'm the real PLATINUM CHICK you used to roll with back in the day. Don't shut me out; I'm not here to judge you. Only thing I want to do is be a friend and offer advice. Give you the support you need." She placed a hand on Yasmina's.

"Alright, but don't pass any judgment. I know I fucked up and things are bad enough as is," Yasmina began telling Selena.

After going into the long-drawn out saga of her life, Selena sat with her mouth agape. She couldn't believe what she was hearing. Not Yasmina, she thought to herself. There's no way she could've done all the things she was saying. Selling drugs, smuggling money, and committing murder! This threw Selena for a loop. As she listened, she couldn't believe Yasmina committed such atrocious acts.

"Yas, what happened when you moved back to Jamaica? I mean, did Scorcher force you into doing this or w…."

"See," Yasmina interrupted, "This is exactly what I was afraid of. That's why I didn't want to tell you back then or now. You're passing judgment. And no, he didn't force me into anything. I'm my own woman and I made the choice on my own." She was clearly upset. "When I first got into the game I was infatuated by the money. It came fast and it was a lot. Over time, one thing led to another and before I knew it, things had gone too far. Murder was involved. In the beginning, I wanted to set my mark, so I created a crew of females called the PLATINUM CHICKS. Things were going good at first, but they started getting out of hand. Now, I'm in too deep and there's no turning back. But I'm not going to prison, Selena," she looked toward her friend. "If the police catch me, they'll have to kill me."

Selena was in tears at hearing her best friend pour her heart out. She knew how hard things were with Yasmina not having her parents around, and now her grandmother was gone. Hearing how she felt if the police caught her, scared Selena. She didn't want to see her friend go to prison, but she definitely didn't want to see her dead.

"So, the guy that murdered Rosa is the same person after you and Scorcher?"

Once Yasmina went into detail about how Shotty Dread looked, a light went off in Selena's head. She gasped deeply.

"We gotta get you some protection. I saw that same guy with two other men at the funeral. They kept looking around like they were searching for someone.

177

Yasmina, you need to get help from the police," Selena said.

"No, I can't go to the police. They'll lock my ass up for sure. You heard what they were saying on the news." Yasmina was shocked that her friend would even think of such. "Scorcher!" she blurted out, "I gotta find him." She explained about the passports and codes to the banks.

"You're not hearing what I'm saying, Yas. At the burial, I saw the short guy with the cane toss something that resembled a picture into the casket as it was being lowered in the ground. What was all that about?"

"Oh my God, that was my picture!" Yasmina sat eyes-wide in shock.

After explaining what scorcher had told her, Selena couldn't believe what was happening. Back in Jamaica, as in many other countries, Voodoo is a worshipped religion. Although some people use the religion for good, many use it for evil. In the case of Shotty Dread, it was being used as evil. The picture was a symbol that marked the individual for certain death. And with relatively all of the people who were in the photo being dead already, Yasmina was next. The severing of the foot was another story. While different people use various symbols to represent power, the severing of the foot is believed to be of the most powerful. A chicken's foot is commonly used in these Voodoo celebrations, but for Shotty Dread, he feels the only reason he's so untouchable is that he defied the religion and took it to another level, chopping off human feet.

After explaining it in detail for nearly twenty minutes, Yasmina could not help crying. If Shotty Dread knew where to find the picture, he probably knew where they were and was watching and waiting, she thought to herself. Selena was persistent in convincing Yasmina to contact a lawyer she knew, and having him hide her until he was captured. Then a deal of some sort could be worked out, but she'd have to do time in prison.

"C'mon Yas, don't be selfish, think about your baby. You know you gotta have medical treatment for the baby. Besides, you can't put yourself through too much more of this. Stress will kill you. Give the baby a chance, at least."

"That's why I'm determined to not let them catch me. How can I be a parent from prison? My chances are better if I run," said Yasmina

"Where are you gonna go? Your picture will be everywhere, plus if that guy found you here in Miami, he can find you anywhere. Have you thought about that?"

After letting the comment linger for a second, Selena told Yasmina that she had to leave. She had an appointment with a client. She promised to come by later and told Yasmina to think rationally. She walked out the door after planting a kiss on Yasmina's forehead.

****

The Blue Ford Mercury sat in the parking lot of Wal-Mart. Because of carelessness, they lost the black Bimmer when the light changed to red. Determined not to lose the vehicle a second time, Shotty Dread ordered his driver to wait until the car came back around. Deep down, he felt that the young lady driving knew Yasmina's whereabouts. Just as he figured, two hours later, the Bimmer pulled up at the same exact stop light. Nudging the driver, he pointed his cane, gesturing for the

179

driver to follow. Riding two car lengths behind, he was able to confirm that it was the right vehicle. The license plate read, **Selena-1**. Removing the machete from it's ivory case, he started wiping the blade down with a smooth cloth. It was the knife that was recently used when he severed Rosa's foot, as well as poncho's. One way or another, Shotty dread figured he'd get the answers he needed, as he tapped the driver, informing him to keep a safe distance.

Preoccupied with her thoughts and unaware of the car following her, Selena drove with no regards of anything suspicious. Thinking to herself, she figured if Yasmina waited too long to make a decision, Shotty Dread was bound to find her. She pulled into the underground parking deck of her complex, without paying any attention to the car that followed closely. She made her way to the door and while inserting the key something hit her and she blacked out. She came to, but her head ached from the big bruised knot on the center of it. She also found that she was gagged, duct tapped, and bound to a chair in her kitchen.

As her eyes locked in on the man walking around smacking the machete in his hands, she realized it was the same guy from the funeral. Fear gripped her.

"Mi ask you one time, no more," he said as he pulled the duct tapped from her lips. "Where's Yasmina?"

Pondering on whether or not to say anything, she knew death was certain either way. In the midst of her indecisiveness, she waited a minute too long before answering. Meaning every word he'd uttered, Shotty Dread raised the machete and one by one popped each button off her shirt, exposing the smoothness of her cleavage. This cause the two other men to gather closer, as each took turns groping her. The sexual harassment went on for minutes, and humiliation was suffered to a large extent. Selena wished they would just kill her instead of imposing such cruelty on her.

As one nibbled on her neck, the other sucked on her breast. Taking in the putrid scent of the men's body, she was on the brink of vomiting as tears trickled down her cheeks. Wanting the torment to stop, she figured she'd speed the process along. As one of the men attempted to kiss her in the mouth, she reacted in hopes that her plan would work. As the thick glob of spit caked the corner of his mouth, his neck snapped away violently. The rage was evident, and just as the back of his hand met her face, smacking her, Shotty Dread intervened.

To see the fear etched across Selena's face as Shotty Dread sized her leg up with the machete, brought delight to the other men's faces. The vicious chop caused blood to spew everywhere. Trying to scream and yell was useless, a firm hand pressed hard against her open mouth, causing her words to be suffocated. Sweat beaded on her face and she was beginning to convulse, but the water that splashed against her face kept her awake, although disoriented. As blood soaked the plush carpet, the house was being thoroughly searched for any clues that would lead to Yasmina. Just as it seemed that all clues had run out, the telephone rang. The caller I.D. held the name Murray Peterson. Placing the receiver to his ear, a voice on the other end said, "Selena, be sure to bring your f....."

"So we meet again," Shotty dread's deep voice vibrated in Yasmina's ear.

"Who is this? Where's Selena?" fear began to grip Yasmina.

"Who you tink'? Mi will get you sooner or later Yasmina," Shotty Dread laughed into the phone.

The next thing heard was the dial tone. Yasmina, shocked, hung the phone up the minute he said his name. She sat on the sofa with her knees under her chin crying. "Another person she loved was murdered because of her," she thought as she trembled in tears. Felicia, seeing the distraught look upon her face, didn't know what to do. It brought sadness to her because she knew that whatever was happening to Yasmina had to have a big impact.

Yasmina was calling Selena to inform her that she'd made her decision. Thinking about the welfare of he baby, she decided to give it a chance at life. In so doing, she was turning herself in to the lawyer friend Selena told her about. But the plans had changed after ghastly hearing Shotty Dread's voice.

Within twenty minutes of receiving the call from Murray, Scorcher made it back to the house. They knew Shotty Dread's next stop would be there, so he convinced them to use plan B. Murray's house in Orlando. He wanted to make sure everyone was well out of danger if and when Shotty Dread came through. Just as before with the hotel, they wiped the place down of any prints, removed all pictures, and tossed any piece of paperwork with names on them into the fire place. There could be no information left that could be used as a paper trail for the Feds or Shotty Dread.

Now that Murray was safely leading the women to another locale, Scorcher went about doing some things of his own. With his cache of weaponry, he stashed guns and knives all about the huge house. He knew it would be an uneven battle but the playing field was even enough because he knew the layout of the house. A minute before placing his last weapon, a creaking sound could be heard downstairs. It was coming from the backdoor of the kitchen. As he crept down the stairwell, he then heard the doorknob of the front door jiggle. So he stopped dead in his tracks. A second later, he could see a head peeping around. Shotty Dread. Crouching behind, were his men to various areas in the house.

Slowly, one of the men advanced up the stairs with his gun in ready position. Each step caused a creaking sound, and Scorcher waited with the huge knife by his side. The last step at the top, a guttural moan escaped the man's mouth as the knife plunged deep into his ribcage. The look upon his face showed the pain he was in, and seconds later, his descent downstairs was noticeable to all. Landing to the bottom of he stairs, face flat, Scorcher watched from above as Shotty Dread and his other Lieutenant scurried to see their fallen comrade. Looking up in the direction of his fallen soldier, Shotty dread let out a horrifying noise. He was letting Scorcher know that killing him would be better than any of the others, then a shot rang out, barely missing him.

The bullet ricocheted off the bookshelf barely missing Scorcher's head by inches. Retuning fire gave him enough time to move to a better hiding position. This allowed him to get a better view of his enemies, they had to come upstairs in order to get him. Barking an order to his lieutenant, Shotty Dread waited for the man to advance up the stairs. Seeing that he wasn't moving, an icy gaze told him that if he didn't move in the next second, his life would be taken. With that, the man slowly advanced to be shot in the head. He landed at the bottom of the stairs and lay crumpled beside his comrade. Pissed, Shotty Dread yelled, "Mi cut your eyes out and watch you die a slow death. Put the gun down and do it like a real rude boy Jamaican. Come now Scorcher, fight like a mon'."

Not even a second later, Scorcher appeared. A 9mm could visibly be seen in his hands, and he cautiously advanced down the stairs. Thinking to himself, he wondered why Shotty Dread didn't think of the others he'd killed. He didn't fight them fair. Raising the gun, two shots caused Shotty Dread to fall to the floor in a heap of blood. The screaming he did was pleasure to Scorcher's ears. It was payback for all the innocent people he'd killed. The machete still in his hands, he cursed every blasphemous word he knew. With a bullet in each leg, somehow Shotty Dread found the strength to stand. Using his cane for balance, he lunged forward swinging the machete wildly at Scorcher. Death was clearly in his eyes. The two fought each other with every once of strength they had left. Suddenly, a wince came from Scorcher as the sharp blade pierced his stomach. Blood oozed out but he didn't stop fighting. To give in now would mean death.

He was in a bad position now. His knife on the floor, not too far away from Shotty Dread but too far to grab, he was defenseless. As Shotty Dread moved in for the kill, Scorcher noticed that he wasn't using the cane and took advantage of the situation. Kicking his leg out was his only attempt at surviving, it connected and sent Shotty Dread tumbling down to the floor. The blade of his machete protruded his clothing. It was embedded deep into his shoulder blade. He had to think fast, he knew he had to have an escape goat. The cops were too hot on their trail. He left a note attached to the door about Shotty Dread, he grabbed all of his weapons and limped to his car. Driving down I-4, he passed more than fifteen police cars, all headed in the direction of where he'd just left.   He connected to I-75, and suddenly freedom was in Orlando. Then it was time for plan C.

19

"A CLEAN SLATE"

Months passed for the three fugitives as the Feds continued their world-wide manhunt. Not having any solid leads to the whereabouts of Scorcher, Murray, or Yasmina, they continued to scour about looking for any clue or clues that would lead them to the trio. Since Scorcher had made it to Orlando safely, they went ahead with the plans they'd made in the event that the Feds found out about them. Although times had been stressful, Yasmina successfully gave birth to their new daughter, Serosa. She'd felt bad about putting Selena and her grandmother in harm's way, and dedicated the name in their memory.

While the TV reporters announced the capture of the serial murderer that chopped off the feet of his victims, the three fugitives went about their way. Plastic and Reconstructive Surgery was being administered. Though Yasmina wasn't fully healed after giving birth, she underwent the procedure, and felt the sooner they were away from him, the better their chances were.

Upon meeting William Earthrain, Scorcher could tell that he wasn't a stable individual. Something wasn't right about him. His character was too polished and he knew that everyone had a hidden agenda. It was just a matter of finding out William's agenda. When Murray purchased the five-bedroom home in the Winterpark section of Orlando, he met his new neighbor the first day he moved in. From a distance, William watched the movers haul all the expensive furniture into the home. He couldn't stop admiring all the expensive vehicles in the driveway. The Mercedes, BMW 740IL, Hummer, and the Range Rover, all sitting on chrome. In his natural way of thinking, he assumed that Murray was some sort of sports star. Besides, what other way could a black man gain such possessions, he thought as he stared over the hedge bushes. This prodded him to walk over and introduce himself.

After giving Murray a brief run down of his life, he started talking about his occupation. One thing led to another and before long, Murray knew about every problem his new neighbor had. This played to his advantage. Listening to him sulk about the divorce he was going through with his wife of twelve years, not able to have kids because of being sterile, and his biggest issue of all, infidelity, Murray began to see the other side of his new neighbor. The weak one.

Although he kept his wife financially happy, she was emotionally sad. With her biological clock ticking, time was running out and she wanted to bare children. She loved William dearly, but she was lonely. All of his time was taken; working with patients all through the night. During his absence and her loneliness, she began surfing the web to find something to help her while he was away. Going into the singles chatrooms, she was curious about what single people talked about. Before long, months had passed and her conversations with Charles were happening on a regular basis. What started out as a friendly curiosity, turned into meetings, and meetings turned into sexual rendezvous.

One night after surgery, William came home depressed and in a funk. He'd lost a patient after doing a Gastric Bypass procedure. Feeling down, he came home wanting to hear the soothing voice of his wife telling him that everything will be all right. Instead, he walked in to hear her screaming, "Oh, Charles, this dick feels so good. Fuck me! Fuck me! Fuck me!" This spectacle drained every ounce of will out of him. To make matters worse, the look in her eyes was one of pleasure as she stared into his as Charles stroked her in the doggy position the entire time. And he was a hugely built black man.

Heart broken and defeated, he went into the basement. Grabbing the remote, he surfed the channels as he rocked back and forth in his chair with tears streaming down his face.

This was one of the many stories he told Murray. The other had to do with his business. His medical practice, which started out to be a very lucrative and successful one, was beginning to crumble. His clients were starting to go elsewhere, as was his desire to be a surgeon. A client of his, a female who'd recently had a breast job done by him, was filing a lawsuit. She claimed that the surgical instruments used weren't sanitized, and an infection caused her to have her left breast amputated. This caused an uproar with the business. However, when the man died while having Gastric By-pass surgery, the collapse of his practice was inevitable.

Negligence was found on his part and his staff for leaving a surgical clamp inside the man's stomach. A $90 million dollar lawsuit caused him to file for chapter 11. His business closed for good the following day. With this information, Murray knew that somewhere along the line William would play a vital part in their survival. But William was thinking the same thing as he relayed all of his information. Murray would be that lifeline that he needed.

With no solid enough leads on Scorcher or Murray, the DEA knew that it would be hard to find them. The photos they did have weren't enough for NCIC to link them with any fingerprints or other photos. The dreadlock wig that Murray wore while in the hotel with Jaheim was a great disguise. Not knowing the process of Plastic Surgery was being done on the fugitives, the Feds were about to lose them forever.

Paying William a million dollars in cash to change their appearances was the best investment they ever made. William was also told that an extra hundred thousand would be added for hush money. For Scorcher, he hoped that a reward wouldn't be announced on TV anytime soon. He felt that William would sell them out at the drop of a dime. Three months had passed and they were in the clear. William stuck to his side of the deal, and they were headed to their new home in Hawaii. It was time for a clean slate.

****

Agent Vincent and Wallace were congratulated by Chief Sculea for catching Shotty Dread. He received the death penalty, b ut there was still a problem. Scorcher, Yasmina, Murray, and Jaheim were still at large. They managed to let them slip away. Although Stacey provided them with information, she was sentenced to life in prison without the possibility of parole. For the two agents, they were demoted to working the desks. However, the Feds weren't going to give up on the chance to catch the trio. They knew that they'd get the break that they needed. And luckily for them, the break came five years later.

20

"A SECOND CHANCE"

AGENT VINCENT and Chief Agent Sculea caught the first flight out departing from LAX. This was the first time in five years that they'd heard anything about Yasmina, Murray, and scorcher, and the possibility of the tip being true was overwhelming.

"What's this guy's name again?" asked Chief Sculea.

Agent Vincent knew this was his chance to make good a situation that he'd blown more than once. Flipping through his note pad he said, "Uh, William Earthgrain, sir."

"If this son of a bitch doesn't bullshit us, we'll get their asses this time around. You can bet your bottom dollar on it."

As the plane touched down onto the runway in Orlando, the two agents gathered their briefcases. This was the biggest break in the case in a long time, and they wanted to get every piece of information they could. Knowing the priority of the case, they were prepared to offer clemency for the capture of the deadly trio. And in William's case, his heinous crime could be swept under the rug. Chief Sculea celebrated as they headed for the county jail.

Seeing the pale and shriveled man sitting in the steel chair, both Agent Vincent and Chief Sculea wondered about his connection to the missing trio. His oversized jumpsuit was two sizes too big and made him look smaller than he really was. The only way they could distinguish that he was older, was by the huge bald patch where hair once stood on his head. Knowing how vital any information retained was, Chief Sculea didn't hesitate. He went straight for the jugular.

"Take a look at these," he slid a few pictures in front of him. "Can you tell me who these people are?"

Taking a hold of each photo and scrutinizing them closely under the thin framed glasses, William started speaking, "Uh yes, but wha…"

"Look you asshole," blared Chief Sculea interrupting him, "We have you for practicing medicine and surgical operations illegally, not to mention murder. If I were you, I'd come forward with any and everything I know. I know you're wondering about a deal, and yes, if you can provide us with enough information to lead to the arrest of these three fugitives, I'll personally see to it that you walk out of here Scott free. No charges, nothing."

Once again browsing through the photos, William was only able to identify one person, Yasmina. The other two males, he'd never seen them before.

"Are you sure you don't recognize the two gentlemen?" Agent Vincent chimed in disbelief.

Shaking his head, William replied, "I'm positive. Look, you guys don't have to yell at me, I'll help you anyway I can. Heck, I'll even give you a sketch to go off, but there's one thing," he held up a finger for emphasis.

"I want to be sure you guys stick to your end of the bargain," he smiled.

Both agents looked puzzled and slightly angered, but the ball was in William's corner. They needed Scorcher, Murray, and Yasmina, and would get them by any means necessary. After Williams's lawyer showed up, papers were drawn and a deal was made. He then informed them where photos of the three fugitives and the newest addition-Serosa, could be found in his home.

For William, this was a blessing in disguise, he thought as he sat at the table. For as long as he could remember, bad things had been happening to him. His wife left him, his business crumbled, and he practically lost his mind. He came from generations of doctors, his father, his grandfather, and him. It was all he knew how to do. This lifestyle enabled him to buy that quarter of a million dollar home that his wife lived in, the two matching Mercedes Benz that she now drove, and a phat bank account. He couldn't imagine himself living below those standards.

Having nothing and using the million dollars Murray had given him, he started an underground practice at his home. The surgery he'd done on Yasmina, Scorcher, and Murray had turned out flawless, so his confidence was restored. Not having any license, he used specific clientele. These were clients who wanted his services regardless of how the news painted him to be. Plus, his prices were well lower than the legal practices around town.

One particular Sunday morning, he received a phone call. It was from one of his clients, a young lady who'd had a few things done in the past. Breast Implants and Botox. She was persuing a modeling career and needed a portfolio at the last minute. Not happy with the extra pounds on her tummy, she wanted a quick tummy tuck done. Something as simple as Liposuction could've been used to remove the unwanted fat, and it would've had less scarring, but William in his high state of mind, opted for another measure. That morning before

192

receiving the call, he'd just finished the last of what was the contents of a half once of cocaine. He'd purchased it a few days before. Still wired, he grudgingly argued with the girl about the horrible scarring a tummy tuck operation would leave. After minutes of protest, she finally gave in. The guaranteed that his Gastric By-Pass Operation would be so precise, she would never be able to tell that she had an operation, was good enough for her to go along with it.

The first stages of the surgery were going well, until something terrible started going wrong. Although sedated, the girl's body started convulsing. Realizing that the hemorrhaging and bleeding wouldn't stop during the operation, he went out of his wits. Everything he tried, failed. With his nose dripping, and sweat soaking his cloak, he couldn't get the sound of the machine flat lining out of his mind. Panic started setting in. He started beating the girl in the chest with his fist, and attempted CPR but couldn't think clear enough to follow the correct steps. His mind was in shambles as he realized he'd killed another person during an operation. Now he had to rid of the body.

One day while sitting in the dayroom of the jail watching America's Most Wanted, he happened to see Yasmina's picture flash across the screen. A re-enactment was on about her dealing drugs and murdering two guys in Myrtle Beach at a Bike Festival. The names Murray and Scorcher were announced but no pictures were shown. Sitting in the chair, he knew these had to be the people he operated on, even though years had passed. It was something about Yasmina's face that made him certain. Feeling that this was a chance to save himself, he dialed up his lawyer. The next couple of days, he was visiting with Chief Sculea and Agent Vincent. His freedom was based solely on their capture.

21

"Karma"

Happy birthday dear Serosa, happy birthday to you, "Yasmina, Scorcher, Felicia, and Murray sang as she blew the five candles out.

Many years had passed as the three fugitives lived in seclusion under new names and identities. Living a life on the run, they had to look over their shoulders constantly, that's why they were very careful as not to fall into any traps set by the law. Still on the FBI's Most Wanted List, they didn't let it hinder them from living a good life. Big homes, luxurious cars, and money was a habit that was hard to break.

To hide themselves, they all assumed their real names, Scorcher aka Anthony Love, and Murray aka Jessie Armstrong. Yasmina was the only other person that had to use an alias, Elizabeth Love. They were now official residents of Honolulu, Hawaii.

Upon arriving on the island, Scorcher noticed that Hip Hop and Reggae music dominated airwaves. It's affect on the people of the island was unbelievable. With an ear for good music, he figured out a way to get established, and a way to clean up their money as well as investing. Real life Entertainment was established, and it had been growing the last couple of years.

Serosa, just a baby when all the drama was going on with her mother and father, didn't know the real history of her parents, and for that matter, her Uncle Jessie and Aunt Felicia.

For a five-year-old, she lived a life that very few kids would ever experience. Not every five-year-old received a diamond tennis bracelet with their initials engraved in it for a birthday gift. She also attended studio sessions with her father, and watched some of the up and coming artists performed.

Wanting to appear as normal citizens with nothing to hide, Yasmina enrolled her in a private school. It was in one of the trendiest parts of Honolulu. She felt that keeping Serosa out of the public schools would limit her exposure to drugs and violence, a part of life that she regretted ever treading. Although they all lived legitimate lives, guns were never too far away. In the world of entertainment, the caliber of people they dealt with was enough cause to merit having a weapon around, but the real issue was of their past. They didn't want to be without one if ever confronted by Feds.

All of this was going on under the watchful eye of a five-year-old. Gun toting, explicit lyrics in songs, and women walking around practically naked. To Yasmina, Serosa was too young to understand any of this, and seeing her emulate it was fun. Little did they know, her infatuation went far beyond what they knew. It was being embedded in her mind.

Every PTA Meeting and school function, Yasmina was there. She became active in every aspect of Serosa's life. Just as traits are passed down in a family, Serosa was a relic of Yasmina when she was young. Feeling good about the outcome of their lives, Yasmina prided herself on the way she was raising her child. And this thought took her back to her parents. Deep down, she knew they wanted the best for her. This was a way to show that what they were instilling, worked. The way that the cards are dealt in society, she

knew Serosa would make it far in the world. She had a
better start than most kids.

****

Chief Sculea arrived at the hotel admiring the
nice weather on the beautiful island. It seemed like a
vacation but this was clearly business, and every second
would be spent combing every inch of the island looking
for the fugitives, he thought, as he looked out the sixth
floor window of the hotel overlooking the beach.

The leads that William provided proved worthy.
A couple months after gathering tidbits of information,
the agents had enough data to pinpoint a precise location
on the island where they might be. The big problem was
finding them on the beachfront of Waikiki that extended
twelve miles. Since it was a very up-to-date and modern
city, Chief Sculea knew that the odds were little to none.

Two months seemed to pass by quickly, and the
agents didn't have any luck with finding a clue in the
first. This caused a lot of frustration. They knew how
clever the trio was at eluding them and being on an island
as large as Hawaii was like being underground in a city
like Atlanta. Figuring it would take a while to track them
down, Chief Sculea told Agent Vincent, "We're gonna
be here for a while."

However, to their surprise, two weeks later they
would receive a big break in the case.

One morning while eating Donuts and drinking a
hot cup of Java, they sat reading the newspapers. This
was something that Chief Sculea did no matter what
state, city, or country he was in. He enjoyed keeping up
with the latest news and events that happened around the
world. While browsing the Real Estate Section,

something caught his eye. It was just a hunch or maybe a long shot, but it piqued his curiosity. The heading read, "Property Subleasing, a three bedroom Townhouse located in the trendy Diamond Head sector." This part of town was known for it's industry. It's the central section of the city and it's Boulevards run the length of the seaport all the way to the airport. Homes are nestled in valleys, making it difficult to find someone in hiding. And Chief Sculea felt that it was this part of town they needed to concentrate on.

Circling the ad with a red marker, he slid the paper across the length of the table.

"What's this?" Agent Vincent biting into a Donut asked.

"Read it," replied Chief Sculea.

Seconds past, and then Agent Vincent said, "Okay, what?" Are you looking to buy property or something?" He couldn't believe the gall of his superior. The entire time he'd been preached about sticking to the manhunt, and not a vacation.

"No, you don't get it, read where it says 'contact one of three owners'." He smiled a huge one.

Following where his superior was leading him, Agent Vincent couldn't help shake his head. Even though it was a long shot, it was the closest clue they had in almost three months. After dialing the number listed, they waited for an answer.

"Hello, Elizabeth speaking," Yasmina said.

"Yes, my name's Bob and I'm calling in reference to the Townhouse you're sub-leasing. My wife and I are here on vacation for four months and we'd like to check the place out," Agent Vincent tried to make his accent more colloquial.

After hanging up the phone, the two agents went to meet the young lady about the apartment. At first, hearing Elizabeth speak, he cold detect a slight accent of some kind. And new it was different from that of the islanders. Remembering what Stacey had told him, he was quite sure it was Yasmina he spoke to. Stacey told him that she could easily switch from English back to her native Jamaican tongue.

When they arrived at the Townhouse, the two agents were surprised with the person answering the door. This young lady didn't look like the photos William showed them of the new Yasmina. Unless she'd bleached her skin like Michael Jackson, then the female who stood before them wasn't her. After inquiring about the owners of the place, it was when they learned that it was owned by three African Americans. Lights immediately went off in both agents' heads.

As a way to stay low key and under the radar, Yasmina never visited anyone inquiring about the property. The only thing she'd do was answer the phone, and that was very seldom. She'd hired the young Hawaiian girl to handle those aspects of the business. Since Lana was taking a Real Estate Course in Community College, it was a good internship for her. It afforded Yasmina enough time to be in Serosa's life in school and at home.

"I think we should put a tail on this girl, see where she leads us," Chief Sculea said as they walked back to their car.

"You took the word right out of my mouth. Did you hear her say three African Americans owned the place?" he looked at his superior and gestured with fingers. "Yasmina, Scorcher, and Murray."

"I bet the accent you heard on the phone was Jamaican too," Chief Sculea retorted.

Discreetly following at a distance, the agents followed Lana back to the Community College, where she disappeared inside. For quite sometime she stayed on the inside, but the agents weren't giving up that easily. It wasn't until 8:30 p.m. that night she came strolling out, arms filled with books. Making it home, she called Yasmina and informed her about the guys who checked out the home. Neither of the two girls thought anything odd about the situation, but it was one fact that was overlooked. When Yasmina answered the phone, the guy said that he and his wife were vacationing, not him and another man.

Friday came and it meant payday for those who worked. Lana pulled into the parking lot of REAL LIFE ENTERTAINMENT unaware of the blue sedan following her. As the two agents watched, she went through the rotating doors and disappeared for about thirty minutes. Not wanting to expose themselves, they waited, not patiently, but they waited. As they talked about different things, their attention was drawn when Lana came out the doors and headed for her Green Honda Civic. Immediately following was a black female and a child that appeared to be no older than five or six. "Bingo! I think we got our girl," Agent Vincent pointed to the two heading for the parking lot. Traffic was congested, but Chief Sculea was able to take a quick glimpse before the City Bus stopped dead in front of their blue sedan. When the bus pulled off, Yasmina was nowhere in sight.

Yasmina was waiting on Lana to arrive at the studio so she could hand her the paycheck that was due to her. Since the central office for the Real Estate

200

Business and the Entertainment Business was located in the same building, it allotted her time to spend with Scorcher, and handling her part of the business as well.

Now that the agents were sure of their fugitives' location, a few phone calls were made. Checks on the studio and property were run, and this pieced everything together for them. NCIC finally had a positive match for the pictures they'd run years ago. Anthony Love and Jessie Armstrong came back as the real names of Scorcher and Murray. It was time to put a plan into action.

22

"HOUR GLASS"

"Team One, what's your position?" Agent Vincent questioned.

"We have the suspects in view," a voice crackled through the walkie-talkie.

"Roger! Team one."

Five months had passed, and the agents continued to compile more and more incriminating information on the fugitive trio. Their surveillance included phone taps, pictures, and fingerprints retrieved at night when everyone left the building. There were even agents infiltrating as artists. Trying everything to secure a solid bust, the Agents attempted to cover every corner possible. No leaf was left unturned.

Chief Sculea was surprised at how the lives of the fugitives had turned out after almost six years. As too often portrayed in movies, the notorious killers and drug lords always seem to come out on top in the end, converting themselves into law-abiding citizens who want for nothing, because they already have it all. "The gall of them," he mumbled to himself as he thought about the $70,000 dollars a year salary he made.

During the following months, Yasmina, Murray nor Scorcher had any inclination that they were being sought by the feds. Life was good, and they were living that dream that they all fought so hard for. Drug Free. The only thing left was to move forward. With the summer ending, school would be starting soon for Serosa. To celebrate her up and coming sixth birthday along with her becoming a second grader, they took her to the country fair.

The place was crowded with thousands of people; spectators, families, and individuals out having fun. Music played as kids enjoyed the rides, and Serosa was in the midst of it all. She was having the time of her life. However, there was a presence amongst them to be unseen, the Feds. Around every corner, two agents were placed. They watched as Scorcher, Yasmina and Murray enjoyed themselves. For scorcher, it was good to see his wife have Fun.. She laughed as she rode the rides with Serosa, and this gave him a sense of pride. He finally had a family. To know that she still loved him despite all the pain he'd put her through, was a love he'd never experienced. That's why at any giving moment, he would risk his own life to save hers. No matter what the cost.

Murray walked down to the basketball tent, he bent down to tie his shoe string and that's when he noticed them. Two agents were standing beside a roller coaster ride holding their radios. Not panicking, he stood up and reached for a basketball; the entire time whispering to Scorcher. Cool and nonchalantly, Scorcher relayed the information to Yasmina. She informed Felicia, and together they headed for the direction of the parking lot, slowly. As she held Serosa's hand tightly and pointed at different things throughout the fairgrounds, her eyes focused on the other agents scattered about.

Just then, three agents started making their way towards Yasmina, Felicia, and Serosa. Speeding the pace of her step, Yasmina almost went into a jogging run, barely dragging Serosa until she picked her up in her arms. Seeing this, Chief Sculea said, "All teams, maneuver back to the parking lot, but don't do anything until I command you."

Adrenaline was rushing. For Murray and Scorcher, they could see that the agents were trying to trap Yasmina, but they weren't going to let that happen. They also knew it was a slim chance that they would make it out alive, but as long as Yasmina made it, it was good enough. Adjusting their waistbands, both men started making their way toward the parking lot.

Chief Sculea didn't want this to happen. For one, too many innocent people were scattered about. Knowing the way Scorcher and Murray think, they knew that a lot of innocent blood would be shed if this went down the wrong way. That in fact, forced him to inform his teams to try to clear out the parking lot. But he was too late. When he made it to the parking lot, he saw that ten of his agents stood with their guns drawn at Yasmina, Serosa, and Felicia. And Scorcher and Murray had the drop on them with the two mini-HK-5 machine guns they held.

"Jessie and Anthony, it's over!" yelled chief Sculea as he stood at a distance. The crowd now in frenzy, started screaming and running for cover. Two unlucky females ran straight into the arms of Murray and Scorcher. Pointing the guns at their heads, Scorcher bellowed, "You have t'ree seconds to let mi family go." The lady cried hysterically as she begged the agents.

"I'm afraid we can't do that, Anthony. You guys are wanted for a string of murders and drug, and we came to do our jobs. C'mon man, think about your child," he pointed to Serosa who was bawling in tears. "She deserves a chance at life."

One of the agents moved two steps beside Yasmina, and Scorcher flinched.

"Hold your fire! Hold your fire!" Yelled Agent Vincent, seeing that Scorcher was about to pull the trigger. "Look, it doesn't have to end this way. I'm sure we ca…"

"Let mi bloodclot family go," Scorcher bellowed once again.

In that split second, Yasmina read the look in Scorcher's eyes. She knew prison wasn't an option for her or him. Though they wanted the best for Serosa, they knew it couldn't be possible if the both of them are locked away. Staring straight into Scorcher's eyes, she spoke "baby, we don't stand a chance. No matter what the cost, I love you and Serosa, and I w…"

****

That evening, every new station on the island ran the top story. The headlines read, **"THE COUNTY FAIR MASSACRE."** It went on to say that five federal agents, including two women held hostage killed in a shootout with three armed and dangerous fugitives. Two of the fugitives, Anthony Love aka Scorcher, and Jessie Armstong aka Murray, were killed also. Numerous innocent by-standers were hospitalized as federal agents tried apprehending the fugitives. They'd been on the run for nearly six years, and a tip led the Feds to the island of Honolulu. Chief Sculea, the head of the investigation was injured, and his partner Agent Vincent was killed when a bullet struck him in the head. Yasmina Powell was taken into custody and charged with murder, along with various drug offenses.

23

"PRODUCT OF SOCIETY"

One year later, Yasmina was sentenced to the Death Penalty. She was to face punishment for Scooter and Hasan, the Federal Agents who lost their lives, and the innocent bystanders who perished also. Upon hearing the testimony of Chief Sculea and the families of the victims, the judge threw the book at her.

When the agents had them cornered in the parking lot, Yasmina did the inevitable. While she made her pleading speech to Scorcher, she took advantage of an opportunity that presented itself. The officer, who inched his way close to her, started letting his guard down when he heard her begging Scorcher to give up. With his hands relaxed around his extended weapon, it was too late to react when she snatched it out of his hand and started firing on other agents. Luckily, he was able to knock her to the ground and retrieve it, but he was too late. Scorcher and Murray started spraying the place. Yasmina was taken into custody, and child services took Serosa. It would be the last time she saw her daughter alive, or would it?"

****

The PLATINUM CHICKS were no more. They were either locked-up or dead, except for Damita. She used the money she'd saved up and opened up a hair salon in Seattle, Washington. With her kids having trust funds and their college tuitions paid in full, the only thing left to do was live under the alias she was now using, Rochelle DeMarcus.

Latoya was killed by the Feds in a shootout and the only member left was Stacey, who was sitting in prison for the rest of her life. Her days were filled with her new love, a Spanish girl named Vida. Yasmina sat on Death Row awaiting her date of execution.

Serosa, now seven years old, had been moved from Foster Home to Foster home. At a young age and experiencing so much, she was traumatized by everything that happened. This caused her to have nightmares and families couldn't put up with her acting out. On one occasion, she was caught behind the house smoking a cigarette. It was immediate grounds for removal. As weeks and months went by, she seemed to get worse. Arguments ensued between her and staff members, and in one instance, she slapped a staff member in the face.

Unable to handle her, the state put her into a juvenile hall for young girls. This place was more like a prison for kids, and to survive, she had to be just as tough as the other kids. One day as she made her way back into her cube, she saw a girl looking through her things. An argument ensued, then a fight, but the staff managed to separate them. Early that morning as the staff did count, they found the girl dead. Her neck slashed from ear to ear. Serosa was charged with murder and sent to Juvenile Hall for teenagers until eighteen. Then it was on to a real prison.

The life that Yasmina was trying to build for Serosa only corrupted her. While being interviewed by a psychiatrist, some fascinating things were discovered.

The interview lasted for about an hour, but the psychiatrist was able to assess her mental capacity to a certain degree. This led to a few questions.

"Okay Serosa, I'm going to ask you one last question, sweetheart." The Psychiatrist tried talking to her in a voice of a mother. "Tell me one thing that you want out of life."

Serosa, with her head cast down to the floor and fiddling with a piece of paper that sat on her lap, looked up. A few seconds later she looked the lady directly in the eyes and said,

"I want the same thing my parents wanted."

Excited about the rare feedback, the evaluator anxiously followed the answer with another question. She liked the progress she was making.

"And what's that sweetheart?" she asked.

Forming an expression that most would consider too serious for a seven year old, she answered.

"I want out….."

A NOVEL FROM THE BESTSELLING AUTHOR OF "MEETING MISS RIGHT" AND "SEXUAL EXPLOITS OF A NYMPHO"

REVISED EDITION

Neglected
SOULS

"Dark alleys, cold and lonely nights just trying to survive... Who can you run to? Neglected Souls made me gasp and grip my heart."
—Rashamba Williams, Best Selling Author of Driven and At The Court's Mercy.

RICHARD JEANTY

Motherhood and the trials of loving too hard and not enough frame this story...The realism of these characters will bring tears to your spirit as you discover the hero in the villain you never saw coming...
Neglected Souls is gritty, hardcore and heart wrenching.
In Stores!!

A NOVEL FROM THE BESTSELLING AUTHOR THAT BROUGHT YOU "NEGLECTED SOULS"

Neglected
NO MORE
THE SEQUEL TO *NEGLECTED SOULS*

RICHARD JEANTY

Jimmy and Nina continue to feel a void in their lives because they haven't a clue about their genealogical make-up. Jimmy falls victims to a life threatening illness and only the right organ donor can save his life. Will the donor be the bridge to reconnect Jimmy and Nina to their biological family? Will Nina be the strength for her brother in his time of need? Will they ever find out what really happened to their mother?
In Stores!!!

Betrayal, lust, lies, murder, deception, sex and tainted love frame this story... Julian Stevens lacks the ambition and freak ability that Miko looks for in a man, but she married him despite his flaws to spite an ex-boyfriend. When Miko least expects it, the old boyfriend shows up and ready to sweep her off her feet again. Suddenly the grass grows greener on the other side, but Miko is not an easily satisfied woman. She wants to have her cake and eat it too. While Miko's doing her own thing, Julian is determined to become everything Miko ever wanted in a man and more, but will he go to extreme lengths to prove he's worthy of Miko's love? Julian Stevens soon finds out that he's capable of being more than he could ever imagine as he embarks on a journey that will change his life forever.

The police in New York and other major cities around the country are
increasingly victimizing black men. The violence has escalated to deadly
force, most of the time without justification. In this controversial book,
noted author Richard Jeanty, tackles the problem of police brutality and
the unfair treatment of Black men at the hands of police in New York City
and the rest of the country. The conflict between the Police and Black
men will continue on a downward spiral until the mayors of every city
hold accountable the abusive members of their police force.
In Stores!!!

212

Just when Darren thinks his relationship with Tina is flourishing, there is yet another hurdle on the road hindering their bliss. Tina saw a therapist for months to deal with her sexual addiction, but now Darren is wondering if she was ever treated completely. Darren has not been taking care of home and Tina's frustrated and agrees to a break-up with Darren. Will Darren lose Tina for good? Will Tina ever realize that Darren is the best man for her?

In Stores!!

213

Ronald Murphy was a player all his life until he and his best friend, Myles, met the women of their dreams during a brief vacation in South Beach, Florida. Sexual Jeopardy is story of trust, betrayal, forgiveness, friendship and hope.

Coming February 2008

Tina develops an insatiable sexual appetite very early in
life. Sheonly loves her boyfriend, Darren, but he's too far
away in college to satisfy her sexual needs.
Tina decides to get buck wild away in college
Will her sexual trysts jeopardize the lives of the men in
her life?

In Stores!!!

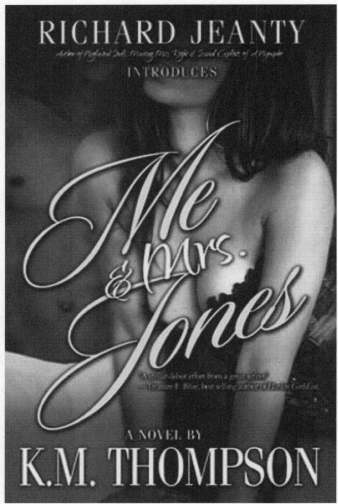

RICHARD JEANTY

INTRODUCES

Me & Mrs. Jones

A NOVEL BY

K.M. THOMPSON

Faith Jones, a woman in her mid-thirties, has given up on ever finding love again until she met her son's best friend, Darius. Faith Jones is walking a thin line of betrayal against her son for the love of Darius. Will Faith allow her emotions to outweigh her common sense?
In Stores!!!

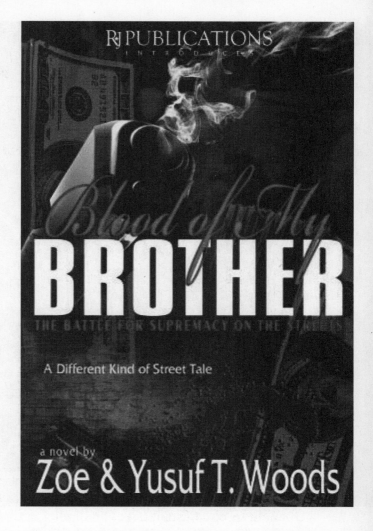

Roc was the man on the streets of Philadelphia, until his younger brother decided it was time to become his own man by wreaking havoc on Roc's crew without any regards for the blood relation they share. Drug, murder, mayhem and the pursuit of happiness can lead to deadly consequences. This story can only be told by a person who has lived it.

In Stores!!!

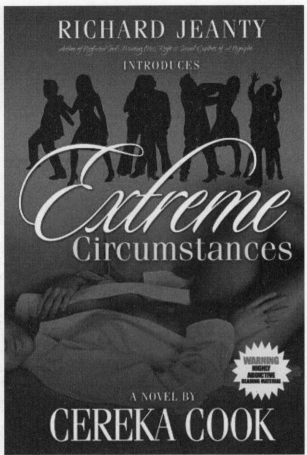

RICHARD JEANTY

INTRODUCES

Extreme
Circumstances

WARNING
HIGHLY
ADDICTIVE
READING MATERIAL

A NOVEL BY

CEREKA COOK

What happens when a devoted woman is betrayed? Come take a ride with Chanel as she takes her boyfriend, Donnell, to circumstances beyond belief after he betrays her trust with his endless infidelities. How long can Chanel's friend, Janai, use her looks to get what she wants from men before it catches up to her? Find out as Janai's gold-digging ways catch up with and she has to face the consequences of her extreme actions.

In Stores!!!

RJ PUBLICATIONS
I N T R O D U C E S

The Evil Side of
MONEY
Street Ministry

A Different Kind of Street Tale

a novel by
JEFF ROBERTSON

Violence, Intimidation and carnage are the order as Nathan and his brother set out to build the most powerful drug empires in Chicago. However, when God comes knocking, Nathan's conscience starts to surface. Will his haunted criminal past get the best of him?
In Stores!!

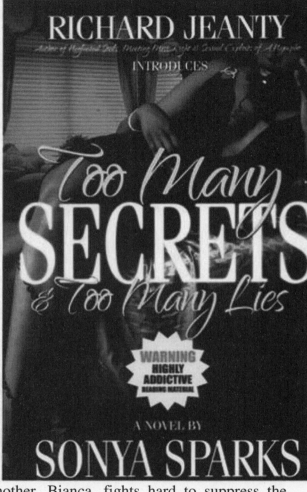

Ashland's mother, Bianca, fights hard to suppress the truth from her daughter because she doesn't want her to marry Jordan, the grandson of an ex-lover she loathes. Ashland soon finds out how cruel and vengeful her mother can be, but what price will Bianca pay for redemption?

In stores!!

Malcolm is a wealthy virgin who decides to conceal his wealth
From the world until he meets the right woman. His wealthy best
friend, Dexter, hides his wealth from no one. Malcolm struggles to
find love in an environment where vanity and materialism are
rampant, while Dexter is getting more than enough of his share of
women. Malcolm needs develop self-esteem and confidence to meet
the right woman and Dexter's confidence is borderline arrogance.
Will bad boys like Dexter continue to take women for a ride?
Or will nice guys like Malcolm continue to finish last?

In Stores!!!

What happens when a woman's devotion to her fiancee is tested weeks before she gets married? What if her fiancee is just hiding behind the veil of ministry to deceive her? Find out as Sean Mitchell takes you on a journey you'll never forget into the lives of Angelica, Titus and Aurelius.

Coming March 2008!!

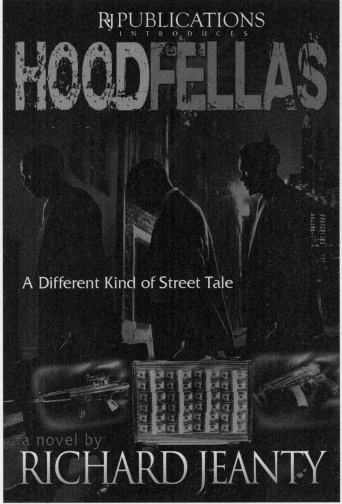

RJ PUBLICATIONS
INTRODUCES
HOODFELLAS

A Different Kind of Street Tale

a novel by
RICHARD JEANTY

When an ex-con finds himself destitute and in dire need
of the basic necessities after he's released from prison, he
turns to what he knows best, crime, but at what cost?
Who's gonna keep the neighborhood safe from his gang
of thugs?

Coming November 2008

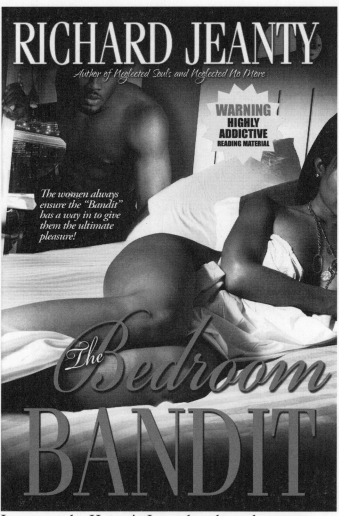

RICHARD JEANTY

Author of Neglected Souls and Neglected No More

WARNING HIGHLY ADDICTIVE READING MATERIAL

The women always ensure the "Bandit" has a way in to give them the ultimate pleasure!

The Bedroom BANDIT

It may not be Hysteria Lane, but these desperate housewives are fed up with their neglecting husbands. Their sexual needs take precedence over the millions of dollars that their husbands bring home every year. These housewives a little TLC provided by the bedroom bandit.
Coming February 2009

PUBLICATIONS
BRINGING EXCITEMENT, FUN AND JOY TO READING

Use this coupon to order by mail

1. Neglected Souls, Richard Jeanty $14.95
2. Neglected No More, Richard Jeanty $14.95
3. Sexual Exploits of Nympho, Richard Jeanty $14.95
4. Meeting Ms. Right's Whip Appeal, Richard Jeanty $14.95
5. Me and Mrs. Jones, K.M Thompson ($14.95) Available
6. Chasin' Satisfaction, W.S Burkett ($14.95) Available
7. Extreme Circumstances, Cereka Cook ($14.95) Available
8. The Most Dangerous Gang In America, R. Jeanty $15.00
9. Sexual Exploits of a Nympho II, Richard Jeanty $15.00
10. Sexual Jeopardy, Richard Jeanty $14.95 Coming: 2/15/ 2008
11. Too Many Secrets, Too Many Lies, Sonya Sparks $15.00
12. Stick And Move, Shawn Black ($15.00) Coming 1/15/ 2008
13. Evil Side Of Money, Jeff Robertson $15.00
14. Cater To Her, W.S Burkett $15.00 Coming 3/30/ 2008
15. Blood of my Brother, Zoe & Ysuf Woods $15.00
16. Hoodfellas, Richard Jeanty $15.00 11/30/2008
17. The Bedroom Bandit, Richard Jeanty $15.00 January 2009

Name_____
Address_____
City_____State_____Zip Code_____

Please send the novels that I have circled above.

Shipping and Handling $1.99
Total Number of Books_____
Total Amount Due_____

This offer is subject to change without notice.

Send check or money order (no cash or CODs) to:
RJ Publications
290 Dune Street
Far Rockaway, NY 11691

For more info please call 718-471-2926, or visit www.rjpublications.com

Please allow 2-3 weeks for delivery

PUBLICATIONS
BRINGING EXCITEMENT, FUN AND JOY TO READING

Use this coupon to order by mail

1. Neglected Souls, Richard Jeanty $14.95
2. Neglected No More, Richard Jeanty $14.95
3. Sexual Exploits of Nympho, Richard Jeanty $14.95
4. Meeting Ms. Right's Whip Appeal, Richard Jeanty $14.95
5. Me and Mrs. Jones, K.M Thompson ($14.95) Available
6. Chasin' Satisfaction, W.S Burkett ($14.95) Available
7. Extreme Circumstances, Cereka Cook ($14.95) Available
8. The Most Dangerous Gang In America, R. Jeanty $15.00
9. Sexual Exploits of a Nympho II, Richard Jeanty $15.00
10. Sexual Jeopardy, Richard Jeanty $14.95 Coming: 2/15/ 2008
11. Too Many Secrets, Too Many Lies, Sonya Sparks $15.00
12. Stick And Move, Shawn Black ($15.00) Coming 1/15/ 2008
13. Evil Side Of Money, Jeff Robertson $15.00
14. Cater To Her, W.S Burkett $15.00 Coming 3/30/ 2008
15. Blood of my Brother, Zoe & Ysuf Woods $15.00
16. Hoodfellas, Richard Jeanty $15.00 11/30/2008
17. The Bedroom Bandit, Richard Jeanty $15.00 January 2009

Name_____
Address_____
City_____State_____Zip Code_____

Please send the novels that I have circled above.

Shipping and Handling $1.99
Total Number of Books_____
Total Amount Due_____

This offer is subject to change without notice.

Send check or money order (no cash or CODs) to:
RJ Publications
290 Dune Street
Far Rockaway, NY 11691

For more info please call 718-471-2926, or visit www.rjpublications.com

Please allow 2-3 weeks for delivery

PUBLICATIONS
BRINGING EXCITEMENT, FUN AND JOY TO READING

Use this coupon to order by mail

1.   Neglected Souls, Richard Jeanty $14.95
2.   Neglected No More, Richard Jeanty $14.95
3.   Sexual Exploits of Nympho, Richard Jeanty $14.95
4.   Meeting Ms. Right's Whip Appeal, Richard Jeanty $14.95
5.   Me and Mrs. Jones, K.M Thompson ($14.95) Available
6.   Chasin' Satisfaction, W.S Burkett ($14.95) Available
7.   Extreme Circumstances, Cereka Cook ($14.95) Available
8.   The Most Dangerous Gang In America, R. Jeanty $15.00
9.   Sexual Exploits of a Nympho II, Richard Jeanty $15.00
10. Sexual Jeopardy, Richard Jeanty $14.95 Coming: 2/15/ 2008
11. Too Many Secrets, Too Many Lies, Sonya Sparks $15.00
12. Stick And Move, Shawn Black ($15.00) Coming 1/15/ 2008
13. Evil Side Of Money, Jeff Robertson $15.00
14. Cater To Her, W.S Burkett $15.00 Coming 3/30/ 2008
15. Blood of my Brother, Zoe & Ysuf Woods $15.00
16. Hoodfellas, Richard Jeanty $15.00 11/30/2008
17. The Bedroom Bandit, Richard Jeanty $15.00 January 2009

Name_____
Address_____
City_____State_____Zip Code_____

Please send the novels that I have circled above.

Shipping and Handling $1.99
Total Number of Books_____
Total Amount Due_____

This offer is subject to change without notice.

Send check or money order (no cash or CODs) to:
RJ Publications
290 Dune Street
Far Rockaway, NY 11691

For more info please call 718-471-2926, or visit www.rjpublications.com

Please allow 2-3 weeks for delivery

PUBLICATIONS
BRINGING EXCITEMENT, FUN AND JOY TO READING

Use this coupon to order by mail

1. Neglected Souls, Richard Jeanty $14.95
2. Neglected No More, Richard Jeanty $14.95
3. Sexual Exploits of Nympho, Richard Jeanty $14.95
4. Meeting Ms. Right's Whip Appeal, Richard Jeanty $14.95
5. Me and Mrs. Jones, K.M Thompson ($14.95) Available
6. Chasin' Satisfaction, W.S Burkett ($14.95) Available
7. Extreme Circumstances, Cereka Cook ($14.95) Available
8. The Most Dangerous Gang In America, R. Jeanty $15.00
9. Sexual Exploits of a Nympho II, Richard Jeanty $15.00
10. Sexual Jeopardy, Richard Jeanty $14.95 Coming: 2/15/ 2008
11. Too Many Secrets, Too Many Lies, Sonya Sparks $15.00
12. Stick And Move, Shawn Black ($15.00) Coming 1/15/ 2008
13. Evil Side Of Money, Jeff Robertson $15.00
14. Cater To Her, W.S Burkett $15.00 Coming 3/30/ 2008
15. Blood of my Brother, Zoe & Ysuf Woods $15.00
16. Hoodfellas, Richard Jeanty $15.00 11/30/2008
17. The Bedroom Bandit, Richard Jeanty $15.00 January 2009

Name_____

Address_____

City_____State_____Zip Code_____

Please send the novels that I have circled above.

Shipping and Handling $1.99
Total Number of Books_____
Total Amount Due_____

This offer is subject to change without notice.

Send check or money order (no cash or CODs) to:
RJ Publications
290 Dune Street
Far Rockaway, NY 11691

For more info please call 718-471-2926, or visit www.rjpublications.com

Please allow 2-3 weeks for delivery

PUBLICATIONS
BRINGING EXCITEMENT, FUN AND JOY TO READING

Use this coupon to order by mail

1. Neglected Souls, Richard Jeanty $14.95
2. Neglected No More, Richard Jeanty $14.95
3. Sexual Exploits of Nympho, Richard Jeanty $14.95
4. Meeting Ms. Right's Whip Appeal, Richard Jeanty $14.95
5. Me and Mrs. Jones, K.M Thompson ($14.95) Available
6. Chasin' Satisfaction, W.S Burkett ($14.95) Available
7. Extreme Circumstances, Cereka Cook ($14.95) Available
8. The Most Dangerous Gang In America, R. Jeanty $15.00
9. Sexual Exploits of a Nympho II, Richard Jeanty $15.00
10. Sexual Jeopardy, Richard Jeanty $14.95 Coming: 2/15/ 2008
11. Too Many Secrets, Too Many Lies, Sonya Sparks $15.00
12. Stick And Move, Shawn Black ($15.00) Coming 1/15/ 2008
13. Evil Side Of Money, Jeff Robertson $15.00
14. Cater To Her, W.S Burkett $15.00 Coming 3/30/ 2008
15. Blood of my Brother, Zoe & Ysuf Woods $15.00
16. Hoodfellas, Richard Jeanty $15.00 11/30/2008
17. The Bedroom Bandit, Richard Jeanty $15.00 January 2009

Name_____
Address_____
City_____State_____Zip Code_____

Please send the novels that I have circled above.

Shipping and Handling $1.99
Total Number of Books_____
Total Amount Due_____

This offer is subject to change without notice.

Send check or money order (no cash or CODs) to:
RJ Publications
290 Dune Street
Far Rockaway, NY 11691

For more info please call 718-471-2926, or visit www.rjpublications.com

Please allow 2-3 weeks for delivery

PUBLICATIONS
BRINGING EXCITEMENT, FUN AND JOY TO READING

Use this coupon to order by mail

1. Neglected Souls, Richard Jeanty $14.95
2. Neglected No More, Richard Jeanty $14.95
3. Sexual Exploits of Nympho, Richard Jeanty $14.95
4. Meeting Ms. Right's Whip Appeal, Richard Jeanty $14.95
5. Me and Mrs. Jones, K.M Thompson ($14.95) Available
6. Chasin' Satisfaction, W.S Burkett ($14.95) Available
7. Extreme Circumstances, Cereka Cook ($14.95) Available
8. The Most Dangerous Gang In America, R. Jeanty $15.00
9. Sexual Exploits of a Nympho II, Richard Jeanty $15.00
10. Sexual Jeopardy, Richard Jeanty $14.95 Coming: 2/15/ 2008
11. Too Many Secrets, Too Many Lies, Sonya Sparks $15.00
12. Stick And Move, Shawn Black ($15.00) Coming 1/15/ 2008
13. Evil Side Of Money, Jeff Robertson $15.00
14. Cater To Her, W.S Burkett $15.00 Coming 3/30/ 2008
15. Blood of my Brother, Zoe & Ysuf Woods $15.00
16. Hoodfellas, Richard Jeanty $15.00 11/30/2008
17. The Bedroom Bandit, Richard Jeanty $15.00 January 2009

Name_____

Address_____

City_____State_____Zip Code_____

Please send the novels that I have circled above.

Shipping and Handling $1.99
Total Number of Books_____
Total Amount Due_____

This offer is subject to change without notice.

Send check or money order (no cash or CODs) to:
RJ Publications
290 Dune Street
Far Rockaway, NY 11691

For more info please call 718-471-2926, or visit www.rjpublications.com

Please allow 2-3 weeks for delivery

PUBLICATIONS
BRINGING EXCITEMENT, FUN AND JOY TO READING

Use this coupon to order by mail

1.   Neglected Souls, Richard Jeanty $14.95
2.   Neglected No More, Richard Jeanty $14.95
3.   Sexual Exploits of Nympho, Richard Jeanty $14.95
4.   Meeting Ms. Right's Whip Appeal, Richard Jeanty $14.95
5.   Me and Mrs. Jones, K.M Thompson ($14.95) Available
6.   Chasin' Satisfaction, W.S Burkett ($14.95) Available
7.   Extreme Circumstances, Cereka Cook ($14.95) Available
8.   The Most Dangerous Gang In America, R. Jeanty $15.00
9.   Sexual Exploits of a Nympho II, Richard Jeanty $15.00
10. Sexual Jeopardy, Richard Jeanty $14.95 Coming: 2/15/ 2008
11. Too Many Secrets, Too Many Lies, Sonya Sparks $15.00
12. Stick And Move, Shawn Black ($15.00) Coming 1/15/ 2008
13. Evil Side Of Money, Jeff Robertson $15.00
14. Cater To Her, W.S Burkett $15.00 Coming 3/30/ 2008
15. Blood of my Brother, Zoe & Ysuf Woods $15.00
16. Hoodfellas, Richard Jeanty $15.00 11/30/2008
17. The Bedroom Bandit, Richard Jeanty $15.00 January 2009

Name_____

Address_____

City_____State_____Zip Code_____

Please send the novels that I have circled above.

Shipping and Handling $1.99
Total Number of Books_____
Total Amount Due_____

This offer is subject to change without notice.

Send check or money order (no cash or CODs) to:
RJ Publications
290 Dune Street
Far Rockaway, NY 11691

For more info please call 718-471-2926, or visit www.rjpublications.com

Please allow 2-3 weeks for delivery

PUBLICATIONS
BRINGING EXCITEMENT, FUN AND JOY TO READING

Use this coupon to order by mail

1. Neglected Souls, Richard Jeanty $14.95
2. Neglected No More, Richard Jeanty $14.95
3. Sexual Exploits of Nympho, Richard Jeanty $14.95
4. Meeting Ms. Right's Whip Appeal, Richard Jeanty $14.95
5. Me and Mrs. Jones, K.M Thompson ($14.95) Available
6. Chasin' Satisfaction, W.S Burkett ($14.95) Available
7. Extreme Circumstances, Cereka Cook ($14.95) Available
8. The Most Dangerous Gang In America, R. Jeanty $15.00
9. Sexual Exploits of a Nympho II, Richard Jeanty $15.00
10. Sexual Jeopardy, Richard Jeanty $14.95 Coming: 2/15/ 2008
11. Too Many Secrets, Too Many Lies, Sonya Sparks $15.00
12. Stick And Move, Shawn Black ($15.00) Coming 1/15/ 2008
13. Evil Side Of Money, Jeff Robertson $15.00
14. Cater To Her, W.S Burkett $15.00 Coming 3/30/ 2008
15. Blood of my Brother, Zoe & Ysuf Woods $15.00
16. Hoodfellas, Richard Jeanty $15.00 11/30/2008
17. The Bedroom Bandit, Richard Jeanty $15.00 January 2009

Name_____
Address_____
City_____State_____Zip Code_____

Please send the novels that I have circled above.

Shipping and Handling $1.99
Total Number of Books_____
Total Amount Due_____

This offer is subject to change without notice.

Send check or money order (no cash or CODs) to:
RJ Publications
290 Dune Street
Far Rockaway, NY 11691

For more info please call 718-471-2926, or visit www.rjpublications.com

Please allow 2-3 weeks for delivery